Sing

Football

(Based on a true story)

Vic Edwards

ISBN: 1505559383
ISBN-13:978-1505559385

Vic Edwards

DEDICATION

To Stephen C. Ragsdale,
Football Coach
of the Giles High School Spartans,
1978-2007

CONTENTS

ACKNOWLEDGMENTS

Many thanks to my wife Sue and my sister Charlotte Duty for their many readings, patience and superb guidance, as well as their insightful editorial skills.

1

LITTLE LEAGUE

They called him Buzz at home because his sister, sixteen months older, couldn't say "Lester" when he was a baby. She couldn't say "Brother" either. When their parents tried to get her to call him Bud, it came out "Buzz". So Buzz he became. At school, all the teachers thought it was appropriate since he had great difficulty sitting still. It seemed nobody remembered his real name was Lester Kirk, named after his great-grandfather. Why should they? He was just Buzz Nobody.

"Buzz, get off your butt! I told you nobody sits down on this team. You're supposed to be paying attention, even if you're on the sideline. Give me three laps around the field."

Coach Michaels turned back to the huddle and gave instructions for the next play. Buzz started running. What difference did it make if he was sitting? He'd never get to play anyway. He was just in the sixth grade and all the starters were seventh-grade boys. Pay attention to what? You couldn't hear the coach from the sidelines. Buzz knew all the plays anyway. He learned them from his brother Grogan, who was now playing fullback for the Pembroke Spartans. Grogan knew everything about football. At least, he thought he did.

Buzz dug his cleats into the turf beside the rest of the stragglers on the sideline as he came to an abrupt halt. He wasn't breathing hard and had hardly broken a sweat. Coach blew his whistle to end a play and caught a glance of Buzz in his peripheral vision.

"Son, I thought I told you to take three laps."

He always called you "Son", just before he got in your face and yelled loud enough to be heard downtown. Buzz had already figured it was for the benefit of the team as much as the poor jock getting the yelling.

Buzz didn't answer. It always made things worse. He could never figure out why answering was back-talking and saying nothing brought on "I asked you a question, Son."

"He did, Coach. I counted them." Coach Richardson was the assistant coach. He was older, but he never had played football. He was Jack's father and just helping out.

"You sure, Coach? That was pretty fast."

"I'm sure, Coach. Counted them."

That was something else that Buzz couldn't figure out. They always called each other "Coach" and never their real name. Sometimes "Coach" got the attention of several adults at the same time.

"Good enough. Pay attention, Buzz. You might want to play this game next year."

He stood up for the rest of the practice. He watched Dewey get tackled time and again as he tried to run the ball through a hole that was never there. The big guys in the middle couldn't block. They just stood up and bunched everything together with the defense in the middle where the hole was supposed to be. Wistfully, he wished the coach would give him a chance to run the ball.

"Larry! I told you and Dusty to double-team. Can't two big first-team linemen move a short, stubby, second-team tackle out of there?" Coach was getting in Larry's face now.

"He just lays down, Coach. We can't move him if he's laying on the ground."

"I don't want excuses. I want him out of the hole. How do you think we're going to ever move the ball if he's laying in the hole? Move him or bury him! Dewey needs somewhere to run."

Coach then turned on Chunk, whose real name was Charles Altizer, a short, stubby, second-teamer. "What're you trying to pull, Son? Think the Vikings are gonna lay down when we come at them? Now, I want to see you charging across that line. You're supposed to want to get to the ball carrier and make a tackle. You ever made a tackle, Son? Well, now is the time. Ok, everybody line up and let's do it again."

Buzz smiled as Chunk took another dive. He wasn't a dummy. The safest place for him was on the ground. Pretty effective, too. After another fifteen minutes the coach gave up, blew the whistle for everybody to gather around, gave the same speech he gave yesterday about not beating anyone, and sent the squad around the field for five laps.

Practice was over. Buzz was the first to finish and started off jogging the two miles home. Most of the other players rushed up to their mother or dad, whoever's turn it happened to be to pick them up. Moms always wiped the sweat and dirt off their faces and bragged about how good they were, and dads smacked them on the headgear as they gave additional coaching instructions. Grogan would probably ride home with Jack. They usually hung around with Stanley and some of the kids from high school. Buzz was glad nobody came to pick him up. It would be embarrassing in front of the coaches.

He saw Allison sitting with Becky on the steps at Becky's house. As he jogged by, he could tell it was girl-talk. One would whisper in the other's ear and then the other would put her hand over her mouth as she giggled and tossed her hair back over her head. Maybe if girls could play football with the boys, they wouldn't sit around and whisper and giggle. He knew what they were talking about. Boys! The cutest this and the greatest that! How so-and-so liked so-and-so, and how so-and-so better not even think about him.

Well, if Allison was not at home then Mom wouldn't be there either. He would have the house to himself. He had the house to himself a lot, now that his mom had gotten a job. She worked late some evenings. That was ok with Buzz, but he worried a little about Allison going off on her own after school or having friends over when nobody was around. She was 13 and finally a teenager. A stupid teenager was what Buzz thought. A big glass of milk and a peanut butter sandwich would be enough until supper time and he would watch whatever he wanted on TV.

Buzz didn't have as long as he thought. About halfway through his show, Mom marched through with a bag of groceries and, without even looking at the TV, shouted for him to turn that "trash" off and go get the rest of the bags. He carried in two more plastic bags of groceries and put everything away. He was happy to see enough cans of vegetables and soup and two gallons of milk to last until Mom got paid again next week. There had been times when he ate at George's house because George's mom threw out more food than Buzz saw at his house in a week. Buzz walked back into the living room and found his mother stretched out on the couch with her bare feet propped up on a cushion.

"Rough day, Mom?"

"Rough enough. I'm gonna give my feet a rest and then I'll fix us a bite to eat."

"That's ok. I had a sandwich and Allison's down the street talking to Becky and Grogan went to Stanley's. Think I'll go shoot some hoops down on the slab."

"You be back before dark. Yell at your sister on your way and tell her to get on home. Both of you ought to be more like Grogan and spend more time on your schoolwork."

"Ok, Mom." Buzz picked up his basketball and eased the screen door close. His mother had been answering with her eyes closed and he knew she would be dozing before he reached the street. With her job and shopping and looking after her kids, they usually had cooked meals only on her days off. After all, Buzz was old enough now to look after himself a little. He wished he could take some of the burden off his mother. The job down at the store didn't pay much, but it did put food on the table. One day, he would make it up to her. He'd buy her anything she wanted.

"ALLISON! Mom said for you to get your butt home. NOW!" he bellowed.

He watched as she waved him off and turned back to finish telling Becky whatever, before she was so rudely interrupted. Buzz dribbled the ball on down the street. It wouldn't matter anyhow. She would be home before their mother woke up.

The slab was full. A lot of the high school boys that didn't play football hung out here or in the parking lot at Kroger's. Here they could prove what great athletes they really were. Sometimes they would take up half of the court or play horse or slam-dunk and leave the other half for others. Today they had enough to go full-court so Buzz moved around to the side of the bank and join several other younger kids to watch.

Every once in a while some player would turn an ankle or get picked up by a carload of friends or just get mad and quit and you might get picked to take his place. Buzz had gotten picked before. He knew how to play with the bigger boys. Don't shoot the ball. Just pass to one of the studs and let him do his thing.

Sure enough. Toby missed a slam and nearly broke his wrist on the rim and left, cursing Patrick for a bad lob. Patrick told him where to go and yelled for Buzz to take his place. Patrick should have been at football practice. He was big and strong and fast. He had been a good tailback on the JV team and then he started missing a lot of school and finally skipped part of last year to move in with his dad up in Richmond. When he came back, he had a car and the best Nike's shoes Buzz had ever seen. He no longer had time for ball, except a pickup game here and there. Buzz was glad he had picked him, and he jumped right in.

The game went on until it got so dark they couldn't see the basket. Buzz was about pooped out. He had made a contribution, though. Several times he had sneaked up behind a player on the other team and stole the ball and passed to Patrick on a fast break. Patrick let him bring the ball up court, also. Even though the other players were older, very few of them were faster than Buzz and he could dribble and pass. He was tough, too. You wouldn't catch him crying because somebody pushed him down on the rough concrete or even occasionally kicked him in the rear when they couldn't catch him after he had stolen the ball. Buzz was tough and you had to be to play with the big boys.

He put his basketball under his arm and headed for home. He would have to put some alcohol on those burning places on his knees. He knew if they scabbed over he would likely bust them loose again playing basketball on the slab. There wasn't much danger of it happening in football practice with him riding the bench.

"Hey, Buzz. Want a ride?"

Patrick had pulled up beside him. The car was already full of sweaty bodies and most of them were pulling on a cigarette or chugging a drink. His mother had told him to stay away from Patrick.

"No, thanks. I'm getting in shape for football. Need to make first team."

Buzz couldn't hear what Patrick said while the others let out a roar of laughter.

The tires squealed as the car leaped forward into the darkness.

2

MAKING THE TEAM

As it turned out, Buzz was wrong about those scabs. The next evening, Dewey broke his collar bone in practice. He had tried to run through the hole where Chunk, playing on defense, had piled the blockers up again and ran his right shoulder smack dab into the helmet of Carl Martin, who had tripped over the same pile from behind. After the coaches had tried to put his shoulder back in place, with Dewey screaming bloody murder, his dad got up from the lawn chair and finally decided to take him to the emergency room to have it checked out. The next day Dewey was in a sling. This worked out great for Dewey, being unable to write or do any homework and having all the Spartan cheerleaders carrying his books and stuff. It worked out better for Buzz. Now was his chance to show what he could do.

"Ok, Buzz. Get in here and let's see if you can run and hold on to the ball at the same time." Coach sounded as though he had just lost the season.

Buzz snapped on his helmet, a size too large, and squeezed into the huddle. Coach called the play.

"Let's try it again, boys. Larry, are you and Dusty going to get our whole darn team wiped out? Right tackle. On two."

Buzz lined up as the tailback in a power I. Coach was determined to run off tackle. Buzz knew Chunk would be on the ground and there wouldn't be a hole to run through. He also knew he had better hold on to the ball. Sixth graders didn't get a second chance.

"DOWN. SET. HUP 1. HUP 2." The quarterback barked out the cadence.

Buzz shot up out of his stance like a sprinter at a track meet. He cradled the ball from the quarterback just as he turned, and headed off tackle. No hole! Buzz planted his left foot and made a right turn. The defensive end had crossed into the backfield and was closing on him. With a hip fake to the outside, Buzz dug in with his right foot and dashed by outstretched grasping hands to the inside. Only Willy was left to beat. The defensive back made the worst mistake. He came at Buzz head on. A jig to the left and another to the right and Willy was falling to his knees. Buzz stopped on the whistle, but he could have made it into the end zone. Not only did he know it, from the way the coaches were looking at each other, with eyebrows raised, they knew it too.

Buzz was the Pembroke Spartans' tailback. He busted the scabs every day and swabbed them every night with alcohol. They would heal after football season and turn into proud battle scars. He didn't jog home after practice anymore. He was too tired. He took his time walking the two miles and practiced holding the football. He tucked one end under his arm pit and wrapped his middle finger around the point of the other end in a deadly grip. Just like the coach had instructed. Occasionally, he would zig and zag across the

road like he was running through a defense.
He would switch the ball to the other side as
he made a cut, making sure he kept his body
between the imaginary tackler and the ball.

Tonight he didn't go to the slab after
supper to play or watch the "pros" shoot
hoops. Tonight was Friday night and his
uncle Jesse picked him up about 6:oo. The
Giles High Spartans were playing Blacksburg
at home. Nobody but kin knew that Jesse was
his uncle, because Buzz just called him Jesse.
Everybody called him Jesse. He had retired
from the railroad and was a World War II
veteran. That's why he went to all of the
home games. He and two other men raised
the flag at all home football games. Buzz
knew that Jesse liked football, too. He was at
every Little League, Eighth Grade, JV, or
Varsity game. He always took his coffee jug
and always bought him and Buzz some
popcorn.

Buzz took the coffee, popcorn, an old
army blanket and found their seats. Jesse
insisted on sitting on the 30-yard line on the
scoreboard end of the field. You could have
sat anywhere you wanted to. Buzz looked
around. As usual, there were less than a

hundred fans watching the Spartans warming up. The PA announcer put a tape recorder up to the mike and Buzz stood up and removed his hat, like Jesse had taught him, as the National Anthem was played. Jesse stood at attention down on the field in his American Legion uniform as his partner raised the flag. Some boys playing tag ball near the flagpole with a toy football were the only distractions. Buzz used to be one of them until Jesse told him the least he could do if he wanted to keep coming to the games was be quiet during the National Anthem. It was the only respectful and proper thing to do.

Jesse poured a cup of coffee and leaned back against the seat behind him to watch the Indians kick off. Patrick and his buddies came lumbering down the sidelines, jabbing and swinging at each other. He noticed Buzz and his uncle and skipped up the bleachers and plopped down beside them.

"How you doing, Jesse? Brought Buzz out to watch the big game, did ya?"

"Evening, Patrick." Jesse didn't care much more for Patrick than Buzz's mother did.

"Big crowd." Patrick was being sarcastic as usual.

"They'll be more when we start winning. Everybody will jump on the bandwagon then." Buzz said.

"And when do you reckon that will happen, Buzz? I bet the Indians'll beat us by twenty."

"Might not happen if a few more would come out for the team." Jesse replied as he took another sip of coffee.

"Wouldn't make any difference. Giles has always been losers. All the other teams schedule them for home-coming. A sure win." Patrick was even smiling, as he rubbed it in.

"Well, I think it's kinda sad when there are more boys in the stands that could be helping the team, than there are on the squad. Don't think you and your buddies got any right to criticize, Patrick." Jesse was getting a little hot and it wasn't from the coffee.

"We got better things to do than play on a losing team. Most of us have a job, you know."

"Yeah. Wouldn't need a job or a car or a lot of money if you were doing what every kid ought to be doing. Going to school, studying, and staying home and helping out your folks like you should. Besides, this is your school, too. Win or lose, you're still from Giles. Putting it down don't change your colors. Kind of hard having pride when you're running away."

Jesse must have laid it on too thick. Patrick just shook his head and got up to go find his buddies.

"Betting five on the Indians," he yelled as he bounced down the steps.

Patrick was right. The Spartans were down two touchdowns by the half. Buzz wished he could dress out. He couldn't be any worse than the fullback playing in the middle of the full-house backfield. He was slow and he put his head down every time he carried the ball into the hole. Of course, there wasn't much of a hole. The two linemen reminded him of Larry and Dusty trying to move

Chunk. Twice he had fumbled, giving Blacksburg a "freebie".

Shakey came over and sat down beside Jesse. He lived up Doe Creek and was one of Jesse's closest friends. They had lived in Giles County most of their lives and would meet some of their other buddies several evenings a week down near the slab at the horse-shoe pits. All of them had retired, most from the railroad, and all of them had a run-down car that they helped each other fix up once in a while. They talked football when they were pitching shoes, fixing cars, or just sitting.

Buzz liked to listen to them. Not that he believed everything he heard. One thing he was sure of was that they were real Spartan fans. It would be nice if the team could win and their pride had something to be proud of. Well, they could come and see the other Spartans, the Pembroke Spartans, play on Monday night. Buzz got up and eased out of the stands. Jesse wouldn't notice now that he had company. Those kids down at the flag pole needed another player.

3

FIRST GAME

Buzz was ready. He had been waiting all his life for this game. His first real football game as a starter. Coach Michaels had decided that his brother Grogan would line up as the fullback with him at tailback in the I formation. Mike Dalton would be the quarterback and Jack would be the power back or flanker. The line had improved, with the help of Grogan. If Larry and Dusty could hold their own then Grogan would lead Buzz through the hole. Coach had agreed if the hole wasn't there then it was ok for Buzz to bounce to the outside and get whatever he could.

Buzz hadn't had a good day at school. His mind just wasn't there. Mrs. Whittaker had lost her patience with him and finally sat him out in the hall to work the twenty math problems at the end of the chapter. Buzz had drawn two pages of X's and O's and every play the Spartans ran. She wasn't pleased.

When he got home he couldn't eat. His stomach was tight as a bow-string. He put his pads in his game pants, cleaned up his shoes, and retied his shoulder pads. Strung as tight as he could get them, they were still too loose. So was his helmet. He stuffed some old newspaper in the top, but that rubbed his head. His mother finally came to his rescue and tied a red bandana around his head with the tail sticking out the back. Grogan laughed and Allison called him "granny". Buzz didn't care. That helmet was going to see some action and he planned on staying in the game.

Grogan and Buzz were dressed and lying in the grass at the ball field long before the rest of the team drifted in. They would meet the coach at the Pembroke Little League field and ride to the game at the high school stadium in the back of Coach Michaels' old pickup truck. Larry and Dusty were rolling down the grassy bank and knocking the legs out from under Chunk and some of the other second team. Grogan met Jack as he got out of his mother's car, and before long they were going one-on-one and head-to-head. Buzz stayed back and watched. He wasn't in the mood to be horsing around.

When the coach finally got there, he blew his whistle and had the team to gather around him in a circle. He went over the game plan. *The Vikings would be bigger than they were, but they put their pants on the same way. They were still just sixth and seventh graders. The winners would be the ones that wanted it the most. It was time to let the city boys know what football was all about. Losing was no fun. It was time to have some fun. Tonight would be the time when all that hard work in practice paid off. Be SPARTANS! Be WINNERS!*

Coach Michaels then lined up the offense and Coach Richardson lined up the defense. The Pembroke Spartans spent the next half-hour walking through every play they had in the playbook. Then they switched and the Spartan defense saw every play the Vikings would run. Chunk and his buddies didn't see anything. They just wanted to get in the truck and go. Their treat would be after the game when the team would stop at Dairy Queen to chow down.

Buzz remembered little of the pre-game warmup and drills. He spent most of the time getting a feel of the Vikings working out in the other end zone. In no time the scoreboard horn sounded and the two teams headed for their sideline. Buzz took a quick look at the stands. There were just as many fans as there had been Friday night, maybe more. It didn't matter. He had a game to play.

The Spartans won the toss of the coin and chose to kick. Buzz lined up in his place as the last man on the right side. When the kick left the tee, he was flying down the field. He never saw Mace coming from his left. The Viking cut him down like a scythe. Buzz hit the ground face first with his face guard mired in the turf and his helmet twisted to the side and him looking through an ear hole. He got up quickly. He straightened his head gear and dug out the grass and dirt wedged in the corners of his face guard. Thank goodness the other Spartans had advanced with a little more caution and tackled the receiver about the forty-five yard line. Buzz kept his eye on Mace as he trotted to the sideline. Buzz didn't play defense, so he would have to wait until the Spartans had the ball. He was counting on seeing more of that particular Viking. He had a score to settle before the whistle sounded.

The Vikings moved the ball down the field. Twice the Spartans held them to a fourth down, but they didn't punt. Each time they were able to get their tailback out on a sweep and block down on Curtis trying to play defensive end. Buzz wished Coach would put him in. He could play defense. At the halfback position he would be fast enough to come up and stop the sweep. The Vikings were now inside their 10-yard line.

"Curtis, watch the outside. Hey, Willie. Come up on the run." Coach Richardson knew what was coming.

Willie came up, but the tailback put on one of Buzz's moves and went around him into the end zone. The scoreboard read 6-0. The two teams lined up for the extra point. Buzz knew it would be the same play. It was

the only thing that had worked. Toss the ball
to the tailback and sweep the right side.
Curtis knew it, too. He saw the split end
looking at him out of the corner of his eye.
When the ball was snapped Curtis met the
crack-back block and glanced off and up field.
He was across the line swarming into the back
field sealing the sweep off from the outside.
The tailback cut back inside and met Larry
who tackled him for a two-yard loss. The
Spartans had prevented the extra point.

Grogan took the following kickoff and
ran it back to the Spartans' 42 yard line. Buzz
was ready. He carried the play in from Coach
Michaels. Fullback dive right. Grogan was
the captain and a seventh-grader. Coach
wanted to settle the team down with a good
solid play up the middle. Buzz was
disappointed, but he figured his time would
come. Let the Vikings clue in on Grogan and
then he would break one. Grogan was tackled
before he got back to the line of scrimmage.
Dusty and Larry had moved their man, but
Mace came charging through the hole and
made the tackle as Mike handed the ball off to
Grogan. Now it was second and twelve.
Buzz was anxious for the call. Coach sent in a
pass play to Curtis out in the flats. Mike

overthrew the ball and the Viking halfback was in the right place at the right time. The ball hit him in the gut and he fell backwards but hung on to the ball. Interception! Despondent, Buzz headed for the sideline.

The Vikings held the ball for three first downs. They had moved inside the Spartans' 20-yard line before the drive stopped. The sweep around the end was going nowhere after Curtis had neutralized the crack-back block. The Spartans took over and Buzz raked his helmet out from under the bench where he had thrown it when he came off the field. He straightened up the padding and readjusted the red bandana as he trotted out to the huddle. Mike brought in the play this time, and again, it was Grogan up the middle. Buzz carried out his fake and turned his head in time to see Mace drag his brother down after a short gain. The next play was fullback left. Again, a short gain.

"Cross-buck on two." Mike whispered the call in the huddle. Buzz's heart pounded.

Buzz was ready. At last, he would get to touch the ball. Grogan would fake the handoff over the left tackle and Mike would

spin and give the ball to Buzz over the right
tackle. He nudged Larry as they broke the
huddle to encourage a big hole to run through.
Down in his three-point stance, Buzz dug a
little extra toehold in the soft turf. Mike had
better be quick. On two, Buzz broke out of
the starting gate, like a thoroughbred at a
racetrack. He tucked his elbows in tight and
held his left forearm parallel to his right to
form a pocket for Mike to place the football in
close to his stomach. As Mike turned and
thrust the ball toward him, he closed down on
it like two big clam shells and with both arms
protecting the ball he headed off tackle. Larry
was lying in the hole. He had been chopped
and the defensive end was closing in from the
right. Nowhere to go. Buzz planted his foot
and cut back to his left and ran into Mike
carrying out his fake. The Vikings swarmed
in to make the kill. Buzz dug himself out
from underneath the pile and walked to the
sideline. The Spartans would have to punt.

At half-time the score was still Vikings
6 and Spartans 0. Coach Michaels had them
sit in a circle down near the goal posts at the
east end of the field. The Vikings were doing
the same at the west goal posts. After Coach

Richardson passed out cups of water, Coach Michaels took over.

"I told you these Vikings would be tough. This looks like practice all over again. Everybody out there running around and nobody doing his job. Looks like a bunch of girls. Maybe I ought to see if the cheerleaders want to play. Mike, can't you throw the ball close to somebody as big as Curtis, not ten yards down the field? Dusty, are you and Larry sure you are Spartans? We don't need to plug up the hole, we need to get those city boys out of the way. Buzz, you got to toughen up a little. Learn to stick it up the field even if there ain't nowhere to go."

Grogan, the captain, was the only one that didn't catch any heat. Coach took the chalkboard from Coach Richardson and started diagramming how they were lined up and how to block for certain plays. Instead of trying to move the bigger Vikings off the line, the plan for the second half was to try to outrun them around the ends. The Spartans would receive the kickoff starting the second half. Coach sent the team jogging back to the bench with a reminder that mommies and daddies and grandparents were in the stands watching. It was time to suck it up and play with some pride.

The Spartans were better the second half. They moved the ball into Viking territory on every possession. Buzz became the workhorse. Only occasionally did Grogan carry the ball and then just to keep the opposition honest. More often he led the sweeps around the ends. The only problem was the Vikings were stringing out the plays and forcing the run to the sidelines. Buzz found himself running out of room or running into Mace when he cut back to the inside.

The Spartan defense was holding their ground, too. Seldom did the Vikings get beyond the Spartans' forty, and they were now punting on fourth down. Willie had saved a touchdown when he had jumped on the Vikings' ball carrier's back and rode him out of bounds down near the 30-yard line. Buzz and all the others not playing defense picked him up off the ground and nearly beat him to death, slapping encouragement on his helmet and shoulder pads. The whole team began to get fired up.

It was the fourth quarter when Coach Michaels called a time-out and came onto the field.

"Ok, men. We are starting to look like a football team. We've been running wide left and wide right and now we're going straight at them. Grogan, I want you to fake a lead around right end, and Mike, you make the pitch to Buzz and follow Grogan. Larry, forget about the end. He'll follow the fake. You block down on the tackle and just seal him off so he can't get back into the hole. Dusty, tap the tackle on your way out, but slide off and see if you can get a piece of Mace. He'll be going with the sweep, and you just need to knock him off stride a little. Buzz, take the pitch and a couple of steps toward the sweep and make that patent cut of yours back inside between the end and tackle. Now, if everybody does his job, we may get at least a first down and have a chance to get into the end zone before time runs out. Ready? Let's show them city boys how Spartans play football."

It sounded good to Buzz. He didn't care much for running forty yards to gain only four or five. The sweeps had worked up a sweat. He didn't care if Dusty got a piece of Mace or not. If he just got the chance to get through the line and take him on head-to-head, would be all he could ask for.

The count was on one. This was going to be a quick play and maybe catch the Vikings back on their heels a little. Buzz took the pitch at full stride. He made his cut as the defensive end lunged to the outside and Larry stuffed his helmet into the belly of the big tackle. He had an opening. He saw Mace brush off Dusty and head over to cut him off at an angle. Buzz led him on. He knew that Mace's momentum would carry him in the direction he was going as Buzz planted his right foot, almost came to a stop as Mace rushed by, cut to his left and headed downfield. The Vikings' safety was trying to recover from the fake sweep, and Buzz turned on the afterburners as he outran him into the end zone.

Vikings 6 and Spartans 6 with two minutes to go. They had to get the extra point. Buzz waited for the call. Bootleg right. The Vikings were set up now. They wouldn't be looking for a run to the outside. Mike faked the crossbuck to Grogan and then to Buzz. He then put the ball on his hip and slipped almost unnoticed around the right end.

The Spartans were now leading 7 to 6. They held the Vikings to one possession and ran out the clock with Grogan diving up the middle. Buzz had won his first football game.

The teams lined up after the game to shake hands. The Spartan fans were now on the sideline waiting to offer their congratulations. Buzz tucked the football under his left arm and marched down the line giving high fives to all the Vikings. Mace offered a regular handshake.

"Nice run, rookie. I'll be ready for that cut-back next time."

"Good game, Mace. Too bad you didn't have a little help out there."

They passed on through the line with both having a little more respect for the other. Buzz walked toward the parking lot and watched as the others were mobbed by their relatives. His mom didn't go to ball games. He knew she was too tired after work and he really didn't care. He didn't like being made over and treated like a little kid anyway.

"Hey, Buzz! Come back here." Coach Michaels hollered across the field.

He was standing out in the middle of the field talking to two other men. Buzz kicked the grass and turned and walked back to the coach. He would rather go get in the truck, drink some water and make his bed for the ride home. Now all the other players would probably get the best spots where you could have something to lean against.

"Buzz, this is Coach Stevens. He coaches the eighth-grade team here at the high school. This is his dad. He coached the Green Wave down at Narrows until he retired a few years ago."

"Good game, Buzz. Coach Michaels tells me you're in the sixth grade." Coach Stevens held out his hand.

Buzz shook hands and looked at the other Coach Stevens, the older man in the wide brim hat. He was about to meet the Legend. Everybody knew about Coach Stevens and the Green Wave. They were only the best football team in the western part of the state. A state championship and two undefeated seasons. Of course this was a little before Buzz's time, when The Coach was still pacing the sidelines. But everybody knew of him, even if they had never seen the Green Wave or the Single Wing offense.

"Howdy, son. You looked good out here tonight. Maybe a natural born tailback." Coming from the Legend, that had to be the ultimate compliment.

Swelling with pride, Buzz shook his hand. He quickly turned loose and gripped the football under his arm. He felt a lot weaker now than he had while running that sweep a thousand times. He had called him a natural born tailback. Well, he did say maybe.

Coach Stevens patted him on the helmet and said he'd see him around. He intended to see all the Little League teams sometime during the season. He was kinda scouting around to see what was coming up to the eighth grade.

"I'll be keeping my eye on you. Keep up the hard work and listen to Coach Michaels here. I expect to see your brother next year."

"See ya." Buzz turned and headed back to the parking lot. Before he went through the gate he looked back at the men. Both coaches were listening to the Legend. He was probably telling them about some young kid he had coached, or how football was different today. Maybe so, but football was football. It didn't matter if you were Spartans or Vikings or Green Wave. Buzz knew he liked the game and he liked to win. Boy, did he ever like to win.

4

A GILES SPATRTAN

The Pembroke Spartans went on to a 6-1 record. The Vikings beat them the second time they met in the Championship game. Buzz was disappointed and wouldn't talk to Grogan for two days. Grogan had fumbled the ball in the Spartans' last drive down the field. Mace's headgear had nearly taken his arm off as well as knocked the football loose. Now the season was over and there was nothing to do but wait for next year. Grogan would be in high school and Buzz was sure to be the ball carrier for the Spartans. He had scored at least two touchdowns against every team they had faced except the Vikings. Mace would be going to Giles along with

Grogan and Carl Martin. Buzz didn't see a lot of challenge left.

The challenges were there, just not in football. Buzz could care less for the rest of the school year. His grades were below average, and when Grogan went to high school there was nobody to push him forward. Several times the next year Buzz found himself in the principal's office. Mr. Stuart Roberts began to lose patience with him and reminded Buzz that in high school there would be no football without more effort toward his school work. Fights with the bigger boys seemed to be an everyday occurrence. Buzz didn't start the fights, but he wouldn't walk away either. Roscoe was the worst. He was a lot bigger than Buzz, and although he didn't play football, he had to prove how tough he was. The attention Buzz got after making the first team from all the other boys, and especially the girls, had crossed a wire somewhere in Roscoe's social life. He wanted Buzz down and out.

His last year as a Pembroke Spartan was the same year that Buzz became known as an athlete. The football team went undefeated and won the County Little League

Championship. He scored at least two touchdowns in every game and had sat out the second half in several games because the Spartans had such a big lead. Coach Michaels knew his horse wouldn't be there next year and wanted to give some of the other boys a good look. Buzz had also given basketball a try. His quickness and ball handling had given his team a big boost. They also won the County Championship even though they had lost three games during the season. With Chris bringing down the rebounds and getting the ball out to Buzz, they became the best fast-break team in the county.

Mr. Stuart had convinced Buzz that there was an advantage in getting better grades and staying out of trouble. Several times his Saturdays were taken as he was invited to go with Chris or Roscoe to watch Tech play. They would pile in the back of Mr. Stuart's Cadillac and go to the University and join 40,000 screaming Hokies to cheer on a good football team. And eat. Any outing with Mr. Stuart meant good eating. Hokie dogs and popcorn at the game and pizza or hamburgers on the way home. Twice that year the whole Spartan team had a cook-out in the back of Mr. Stuart's yard.

Jesse and Buzz were at every Giles home game. They even went to some of the away games. Buzz figured that all the fans could have fit into a couple of school buses. Mostly moms and dads. The varsity and JV teams had a tough year and once again ended with a losing season.

The eighth-grade team was better with a 7-1 record. They were hardnosed and in good shape. Coach Stevens had found a hill behind the practice field that ran straight up for about thirty yards, and each practice ended with ten on the hill. The team seemed to have fun even though they did practice hard. Grogan had done well as fullback and Mike completed three passes for touchdowns.

Mace was the most talked about among the players. Grogan had come home and told tales that Buzz had great doubts about. Like Mace wouldn't wash his jersey unless they lost a game and went four whole weeks with a stinking jersey. Coach Stevens made him hang it in the shower room. Coach ran the show and wouldn't put up with foolishness, but he could appreciate a little individuality.

Buzz certainly hoped so. He had worried a little about what the coach might say about his bandana. He had worn it at every game in little league, and like all great athletes with superstitions, it was now his token. He had taken a lot of smart remarks from his teammates and some serious jabs from the other teams in his first year, but now they considered it part of his uniform.

Buzz shouldn't have worried. Coach Stevens never noticed, or at least never mentioned it. None of the other players gave him a second look, but of course he had played with or against them all as little leaguers. Eighth grade was different, and they all had more important things on their minds.

Going to class for fifty minutes and getting five-minute breaks between was something they really enjoyed. Not the classes, but the breaks! He and Chris became good friends. Roscoe would sometimes join them in the alcove between the lockers at break time, and they would watch the girls, talk about what happened to Roscoe in home room, watch some girls, debate the possibilities of the best math class, avoid the bigger and meaner upperclassmen who wanted to cram their little bodies into a smaller locker, and watch some more girls until the last second before the tardy bell.

Football was the same, or almost. The players were bigger and the other high school teams tougher than Buzz had faced before. They hit harder and ran more complicated offenses. Buzz found more bruises and more scrapes to rub down with alcohol. Coach Stevens seem to appreciate his ability as a running back and built his offense around Buzz and Matney. Steve Charles, Rowdy Smith, and Timmy were the stars from King Johnston Elementary. Gordon Matney and Jack Wiggins were the best and fastest backs, next to Buzz, to come out of Pembroke Elementary school. Buzz and the Spartans had beaten the Vikings and Lions of Pearisburg for the county championship, and Coach had watched them play several games in the past two years. He had a plan.

5

SINGLE-WING FORMATION

Football practice started in August before the school year and the sessions were now lasting almost two hours after school. Each day, after warm-ups, the squad would spend about an hour or more on offense and one-half to three quarters of an hour on defense, hit the eight-man sled, run special teams, practice the kicking drill, and end up running the hill. In special teams, Buzz and the other backs and ends would run through all the plays and all the passing routes. If they got a little careless, they would spend an extra session running though the plays again. It appeared Coach Stevens would take nothing but perfection.

Halfway through the season and the eighth-grade Spartans' record with four wins and one loss, Coach introduced a few plays of a new offense. Buzz had never run anything except the power-I or the full-house T formation. It was new to the team, but Buzz knew he had seen something like it before. Coach brought Bruce Farley from the left tackle position and moved him over to the right side between the tackle and right end. He explained to the team that this was an unbalanced line. More men on the right of center than on the left. Made sense. He then moved the quarterback out from under center and lined him up behind the left tackle on the right side. Then he took Gordon Matney over and put him in position one step outside of the end and two steps back from the line of scrimmage. Everybody was looking at everybody.

"This is called the Single Wing offense." Coach Stevens said with his hands on his hips, and a smile showing his pleasure that everyone was still in their place.

"Who takes the snap, Coach?" Buzz was only hoping.

"You do. Some of the time. You're the tailback or the number four man. Sometimes it will be snapped to Jack Wiggin, and he's the number three man."

The picture was coming back to Buzz. He remembered the tape that Jesse had brought home two years ago after Buzz had gone home and bragged about meeting The Coach. Several years ago Coach Stevens' dad had run the Single Wing with the Green Wave down at Narrows. Buzz wasn't sure about this. Nobody ran the single wing offense anymore. Jesse had told him it was used a lot when he was a boy. And that was a long time ago. Teams today depended on a good passing game and counted on the Power-I to run the ball. Coach was probably just fooling around a little bit.

Buzz watched as the coach moved all the players that were not lined up in the offense to the other side of the ball so they could get a better look at the formation. He showed Buzz and Wiggin how to line up with each other and how far back from center. He showed them how to flex their knees and bend forward and put their hands on or near their knees. It felt awkward to Buzz. Coach then put Gordon in a three-point stance like the linemen and told the quarterback to get in a stance like Buzz and Matney. He walked around and looked it all over while the players froze like statues.

"Dean, see if you can make a one-handed snap to Buzz."

The ball bounced twice before it hit Buzz on his foot.

"Try it again. You want to aim between Buzz and Jack and just above the knee. Buzz, you step with your right foot toward Jack as you catch the ball. Remember, we want to be in full motion with the snap."

This time the ball sailed over Buzz's head. The next snap Buzz dropped. After several attempts with little success, the smile faded from the coach's face.

"Ok, maybe this is too difficult for eighth graders. I guess the ball has to be placed in your hands before you can hang on to it. Steve, get back under center, and let's get ready for the Indians Thursday night. But, I want the backs, ends, and centers to stay after practice until we get this right."

The rest of practice was rough. Coach was in a bad mood and the tension caused a lot of things to go wrong. Buzz kept running the tape he had seen through his mind. It hadn't seemed that difficult for the Green Wave. And he really did want to give it a try, seeing that he might be getting the ball a lot more often. If he could catch and hold on to it.

The remainder of the season went pretty much the same way. The varsity and JV teams struggling to win a game, and the eighth grade Spartans whipping up on everybody. The last two games were played at home, and the crowd seemed to be a little bigger on Thursday night for the eighth grade game and spilled over for the JV game. The word had gotten out, according to Jesse, that Coach Stevens had been practicing the Single-Wing offense and a few old-timers were out to pass judgment. They were disappointed when the games ended without any Single-Wing plays being run. They didn't know the coach, yet. When it was ready, they would see it.

Jesse and Buzz were again in their seats for the Varsity game on Friday night. The final game of the season was against Galax, one of the teams in the New River District that Giles was favored to beat, but just by a little. Jesse was more disappointed in the attendance than usual.

"Buzz, what's wrong with the school spirit around here?"

"I don't know. Not too many people interested in football, I guess."

"That ain't it, Son. A lot of folks played in high school a few years ago. They watch it every weekend on TV and lots go to the college games. If more boys would come out for the JV and varsity, maybe we could win more games."

"They won't, Jesse. Some of the eighth graders are already talking about not playing JV, and I know a lot of the older guys are planning on getting jobs after school, so they ain't going on to varsity."

"But why, Buzz? Why can't they wait until they graduate to get a job? They can work the rest of their lives. Believe me, they'll look back and wish they had had some fun when they could have."

"Some of the guys don't think it's so much fun now. They come out here and work their butts off, and who really cares?" Buzz was getting a little fed up with blaming it all on the team. He planned to play and wished a lot of the others would, but when he looked around at the small crowd, he couldn't blame them much.

"I care. At least a lot more mommies and daddies would be out here if their boys went out for the team."

"A lot of mommies can't and a lot of daddies just don't give a s---."

"Watch your mouth, Son! Your mother wouldn't even let me bring you to a game if she knew I let you talk like that."

"I'm sorry, Jesse. It just slipped out. Don't mean it ain't true, though."

Buzz didn't want to go play with the other boys in the end zone. He sat with Jesse until half-time. Shakey came by and the two old men walked down to the concession stand to get some fresh coffee. Buzz watched the band for the first time. They were pretty shabby, too. He was sure the band director felt the same way Jesse did. "If only the students would get interested in the early grades and stay with the program until they graduated," Buzz could almost hear him say.

"Brought you some popcorn, Buzz." Jesse handed the bag to him and Shakey sat down beside them.

Buzz munched on the corn as the second half got under way. The conversation with Jesse had put a damper on the whole game. Buzz couldn't remember much of what had happened in the first half. He only knew the Spartans were down by two touchdowns.

"Buzz, Jesse tells me the boys don't have a lot of fun playing football. You mean all the girls don't hang around the jocks like they did at our high school?"

Buzz looked over at Shakey. He was serious. No smile or sarcastic grin or nothing. He just plain didn't understand.

"Shakey, it's just not the thing at Giles High School. You're cool if you got some wheels and some time to spend with a girl. Look out there! Who would be dying to spend a minute with Benny Fargo? He just happens to have the rushing record here at Giles. Now take a look up on the top row behind you. The biggest, strongest, and fastest guys in school are sitting up there with some of the prettiest girls. You think they're here to cheer on those heroes down on the field? They don't even know who's winning the game. They're only here because that's the only way the girls can get out of the house for a while."

"How about all the publicity and stuff?" Jesse wouldn't let it die.

"What publicity? The Green Wave gets all the write-ups in the county paper. We might get listed on the back page if we don't get whipped too badly. Oh, we get a little notice when we play Blacksburg, but not the kind we would usually want."

Shakey shook his head. "What about in the school? Pep rallies and bulletin boards and morning announcements and such?"

Buzz got up to leave. He didn't talk back to elders, but he couldn't take any more of this.

"You guys just don't get it. Pep rallies, bulletins, and announcements are for winners. There ain't no band wagon to jump on!"

Jesse and Shakey let him go without any more questions. They weren't enjoying the game either. Their minds were trying to piece it all together. It just wasn't the way it should be. Maybe Buzz and his class could hang in there.

Buzz helped pack away all the equipment near the end of October. He hated to see the season end. They had a good team and a good coach and a winning record of 7-1. It wouldn't be the same next year with the ninth and tenth graders on JV and a new coach. He hoped most of the guys would keep playing football. Most of them were good friends.

He let Chris talk him into playing basketball. He had played in Little League and knew he was good enough to make the cut, but he really wanted to lift weights during the winter and try to build up some bulk and get a lot stronger for football next season. Chris pointed out that the JV football coach was going to coach the eighth-grade basketball team and a lot of the players were going out. They could have a good team and Coach Lowery wasn't too serious about basketball. They could have some fun.

They did. The eighth-grade Spartans went undefeated. Buzz impressed the varsity coach enough that he asked Buzz to consider forgetting about football and concentrating on basketball during the off-season. He wanted a group of the underclassmen to come into the gym after school and, in the summer, to shoot around and work on some skills. Buzz didn't even consider the suggestion. He had pretty much decided on the reverse and working off-season on getting bigger, stronger, and faster for football.

The rest of the year was pretty dull. Buzz hit the books enough to keep a two-point average, stayed out of trouble, and was promoted to the ninth grade. He was now a freshman. A real Giles High School Spartan. He loved that name and was one of few that seemed to be proud to say they were a Spartan. He even looked it up in the dictionary and the encyclopedia and found out what brave warriors they had been. If only

Giles could live up to their name, there would be hell to pay on any athletic field.

At home, Buzz helped his mother as much as he could, ignored Allison and her giggling friend Becky, and stayed out of brother Grogan's way. Most of the time he was on the slab playing round ball or playing touch football down at the park. Sometimes it was well after dark when he came home. He would grab a bite to eat and go to his room. His mother had too much on her hands to nag him about anything and he knew if he stayed out of trouble and helped out around the house now and then, he could pretty much come and go as he pleased. Mr. Stuart gave him a used weight-lifting bar and weights he had bought at a flea market, and each night Buzz would bench press three sets of ten repetitions while lying across his bed.

6

NEW HEAD COACH

The surprise came in August. Not that football season was here, but that a change had occurred at Giles. The head varsity football coach, Coach Bailey, had taken a new job and Coach Stevens had been chosen to replace him. Buzz was elated! He didn't have anything against Coach Bailey, but he had played for Coach Stevens. It might be another year, but he would be able to play for him again. Buzz felt that things might be different with Coach Stevens. Little did he know.

The first day of practice was different. The JV and eighth-grade coaches told the boys to meet in the PE classroom before they put on their equipment. When they got there the seats were all taken by the varsity, so they stood around the walls and some sat on the floor near the front. Coach Stevens took the floor and took control.

"I'm Coach Stevens, and the head coach of Spartan football. Not just the varsity. All of you are here to play Spartan football. Not eighth-grade or junior varsity, or varsity, but Spartan football. I and the other coaches are going to dedicate every ounce of energy we have to you and our football program. We expect you to do the same.

"Men, this is not going to be easy. We might lose every game we play this year, but I guarantee you, if you'll stick in there, we'll win more than we lose. We have a lot to learn and a long way to go. We're going to run a new offense to most of you, and, when we perfect it, we'll have the most powerful running game in football. We are going to start it at every level. Little League, eighth-grade, JV, and Varsity. It is called the Single-Wing offense, and it's been around since your grandfathers played the game. My dad ran the Single-Wing when he coached the Green

Wave and had several undefeated seasons. I believe in it, and so will you.

"Now, by the coach's count, you make up a high school squad of about fifty men. We should have that many on the varsity alone. A lot of guys that could and should be here aren't. That's their loss."

Coach paused and looked around the room. He picked up a yardstick lying on the desk and tapped it a couple of times. With a final sharp bang to the desk, he continued.

"It's our loss, too. To have a good program, we need participation. We want every boy in the school. Guys that may never get into a game can help us. And we can help them. How many of you have played on a winning team?"

Several hands from last year's eighth-grade team went up. Some of the players who sat on the bench didn't raise their hands.

"Feels good, don't it? How many of you sat on the bench of a winning team or played on the second team against the first team every day in practice?"

More hands went up.

"Still felt good, didn't it. Enthusiasm, dedication, hard work, and pride are never a loser."

Coach paused again. Buzz looked around the room. It was sinking in. Nobody was horsing around or looking bored. They were all glued to the coach.

"We're ready to get to work. Every coach here is a teacher, first. We don't expect you to show up and win football games. You have to know what to do, first. Second, you have to know how to do it. And finally, with practice, you have to be able to do it. We'll spend a lot of time on the first two and show you, and we'll spend even more time on getting able to do it right. Coach Lowery will take the JV and Coaches Erwin and Kirby will take the eighth grade. Let's go see what it takes to be Spartans."

Buzz's first skull session was over. The three teams went to their separate practice fields. The Varsity had the biggest field with goal posts on one end. The JV practiced on the half grass and half rocky smaller field that dropped off at one end straight down about 80 feet to a fence that separated a cow pasture from the school grounds. The eighth-grade got to practice on the baseball field. The Junior Varsity only had fourteen of their original 24 players because Coach Stevens had pulled up most of the sophomores to Varsity to have enough to scrimmage. Most of the team had to go both ways, and Buzz was the left corner-back on defense as well as the tailback on offense. They had to run their offense with blocking dummies as defensive men. When the team worked on defense, they would go half line. Coach Lowery would be the quarterback for the visiting team and they would run all the plays on the right side of center for a while and then switch over and run all the plays on the left side.

Coach would give them a break about the middle of practice and have them throw rocks off the field. He cautioned the guys about throwing any rocks at the cows, but as soon as his back was turned Chris or Rowdy would scatter the herd. After about a week the cows were always grazing on the far side of the pasture during football practice.

The JV had more success with the new offense than the Varsity. They also won more games. During the preseason Buzz and Gordon Matney got to go with the Varsity when they scrimmaged Grundy and Graham. They didn't dress out, but helped the managers with the equipment and water detail. They also helped some of the wounded Spartans off the field. Both games were a disaster. Coach Stevens tried to fire up his charges at halftime.

"Men, we don't look any better against the G-men than we did last week against the Golden Wave of Grundy. You're making them look like pros. They're just high school kids like you are. You gonna just lay down and quit?

"Well, I'm not. If I have to, I'll dress out Buzz and Gordon over there and put in the managers."

Coach gave them hell for a few minutes. Then, just before he crossed that line between getting them mad and determined, and before they became humiliated and defeated, he lightened up.

"You know, my neck is getting stiff from looking over my head to watch another extra point sail through the uprights. Let's see if we can slow them down a little. We have the ball on offense for the first session. Instead of hitting them off tackle in the four-and-six hole, we'll run thirty-two buck with Timmy and come back with forty-three with Fonzie. Now, Fonzie, when you get through the three hole, turn on the afterburners. They don't have a man on their team that can catch you.

"Let's get back out there and show them we are Spartans. Also, I don't want you to drop me off at the hospital on the way back to get my neck fixed."

The team was disappointed, but they weren't down. Every member had scratches and bruises to show he had battled with everything he had. Buzz knew that Coach was concerned. The G-men were not just high school kids like the Spartans. They were playing mostly seniors while Coach was sending in sophomores and juniors. They might be putting their britches on one leg at a time, but they were pretty big legs.

Coach Stevens was saved from the hospital. The single-wing deception on the toss-sweep and the reverse did score a couple of touchdowns. The Spartans held on defense and the G-men were only able to score once more. What Buzz didn't notice was the second and third stringers for Graham getting a chance to show what they had.

After the scrimmage, Coach didn't smile much and he let them know they had a lot of work to do if they were to win a game all season. But, like the end of each practice, he also left them feeling better about themselves. More than once he had reminded them that without a little bitter in life you would never know how good the sweet could be. They had let the G-men know they were in a game, and that next year the Spartans would be back and things would be different. Coach rubbed the back of his neck.

"I'm feeling better. Let's get back to Giles and get ready for Blacksburg."

The season for the Spartans didn't get much better. They won two out of the ten, and the gossip was the same from the non-fans. Patrick and his cronies would hit on the younger players with "I told you so". The crowd was not much larger and Jesse and

Shakey were still shaking their heads. They were wondering if it would ever change. Could Giles ever be a winner? Why didn't the boys come out for the team? Why didn't they care? Where was the pride? The school spirit? The school jackets?

"You don't see a lot of school colors, do you, Jesse?"

"Nope."

"Not a lot of fans, either."

"Nope."

"Let's stop by the Cafe, Jesse. Maybe hear what the Celco gang has to say about the game and down a few spirits."

"That's the only way this town gets any spirit. You know I don't drink anymore, Shakey. The only thing that gang will be talking about is deer hunting. I guess I could stand a Coke, maybe. We ought to be playing football through the hunting season and filling up the stands for the playoffs instead of sitting on some ridge waiting to ambush a defenseless deer."

Jesse pulled up to the curb beside the Cafe. A car was just leaving and there were no parking spots left on the street. He saw several vehicles in the parking lot in back as he got out and headed for the beer joint.

"What's going on tonight, Shakey?"

"Don't know, Jesse. Never seen this many cars here before. Maybe something at the courthouse."

"Not this late. Must be tanking up for the big day in the woods tomorrow. Monday is opening day, and I guess they will be scouting out that one-and-only deer stand miles back in the mountain. Old as most of them are, you'd think they would know by now that the deer can walk and will be all over the mountain. One place should be as good as another."

Jesse found a stool vacant in the corner by the bar and Shakey stood by him, leaning up against the wall with one foot on the rail. Jesse ordered a coke and a Bud for his longtime friend. Looking around, he could see that the place was nearly full. Ralph, a Spartan fan, win or lose, and a school bus driver from Big Stoney Creek, was sitting on the stool next to him.

"Lost another one, didn't we, Ralph?"

"Yeah. That's ok. We're still young. It'll be different next year, Jesse."

"Think so? Seems like I've heard that before."

"It's different, Jesse. Our time is coming. Most of these guys in here are heading for the mountains tonight to camp out, drink a few more, and tromp through the woods all weekend. You know why they're still here?"

"Nope. I don't recall seeing many at the game."

"Listen. They are all talking about the game. Well, not about the game, but about the Single-wing. Those guys over there at that table are talking to Bob, who was at the game. They are from Narrows and every time Bob describes a play they come back with how it should have been run and how The Coach was probably the only one that would ever be successful with the Wing."

"They know Coach Stevens is The Coach's son?"

"Yeah, they know. Those good old boys from down the river will never be convinced that Coach Stevens will ever be able to walk in his daddy's shoes. That's why next year is going to be different. This year was just the wake-up call."

"How do you figure that, Ralph?"

"See that table over there?" Ralph was pointing to the table near the window.

"Yeah."

"All those guys live in or around Pearisburg. Their kids go to Giles. Some of them don't go to football games, but they are mad as the dickens over what they are hearing down at Celco. They have to work with those boys from Narrows and it never mattered before about the Green Wave beating us and all the bragging that went on. But now the Narrows men are calling Coach Stevens a traitor and how he'll come running back home after he's gotten his tail whipped a few times."

"He won't." Jesse took a sip of Coke.

"No way." said Ralph. "Coach Stevens will do his best to beat his dad's old team, but he wouldn't want to go back there and compete with his tradition or steal any of his thunder, you might say. No, young coach Stevens will be here for a long time and build his own tradition is my guess."

Jesse looked around and listened. The talk really was football. Not hunting nor the potato crop nor overtime at the plant nor the weather, but football. A rush of adrenalin was tingling his hairline around the back of his neck. Maybe spirit and pride wasn't dead. Maybe all the community needed was a little challenge or a push. Narrows was providing more than a coach, and maybe pushing a little too far. Those hunters should know how a mommy bear reacts when cornered.

Jesse and Shakey stayed until closing. A lot longer than Jesse would ever have imagined. He had a spring in his step as they headed back to the car, and it wasn't the Coke. Coach Stevens might need a little help, and he knew for the first time that he wouldn't be the only one stepping forward.

7

PRIDE AND PARTICIPATION

Coach Stevens spent a rough winter and spring alone in his house after school. He was fired up about building a good football program at Giles and had already spent many hours of non-school time reviewing films of the past season. He had reviewed films of his dad's career over and over again. He had charted every play and analyzed every position. He had gone out to the gym on weekends and set up dummies and parking cones and spaced off the linemen to the inch. He knew how wide he wanted the splits in the line and how far back the backs would take their stance. He diagrammed every play, every double-team, every trap, and every passing route. He felt good and confident that his time spent would produce a winner at Giles. Until he went home, sat down in his recliner, and thought of past seasons and coaches at Giles.

The Spartans had had five winning seasons in the past twenty years. They had averaged two years per coach. Some of the coaches had been honored football players in college and had gone on to be successful at other schools. The student participation in all sports had been poor. Sometimes the eighth-grade and junior varsity had to practice against each other to have an offense and a defense. It could have been the same for the varsity this past year if he hadn't pulled up enough underclassmen to fill a squad. The school seemed to be apathetic and the community outlook was definitely negative.

Could he change the negatives to positives? Should a coach get involved in non-coaching activities? Would he have time? Why couldn't he just coach? If they didn't want to play, what could he do? One thing he knew was if they didn't show up he couldn't coach them. Another thing he could do was put together a total program. He would meet with his assistant coaches during the off-season and do some brainstorming and come up with a plan. He certainly didn't intend to sit on his butt and accept that this was the way it had always been.

After the Christmas holidays, he called in his assistant coaches and did a complete inventory of all football equipment. The equipment room was a wreck. They pulled everything out in the middle of the gym floor and starting matching up shoes, sorting pants and helmets by size, and making a pile of hand-me-downs for the junior varsity. They didn't throw away much. The principal and athletic director had informed him when he was hired that he would be operating on a shoestring.

"Hey, Coach. I've got two left shoes, size 10, with no match. Pretty bad shape. Want me to toss them?" Coach Lowery was tying matches together by the shoestrings and stacking them on a shelf over his head.

"Yeah, Coach. Use your best judgment on those worn-out ones. We'll send down to the JV any good odd shoes. They may have a match."

Coach Stevens was matching up jerseys. A lot of the blue game jerseys were not only well-worn, but also faded as well. He sure wished they could afford to buy new ones. Maybe a red color. The school colors were red, white, and blue. 'Go Big Red' wouldn't be abandoning any school tradition. What tradition?

"Hey, Coach Edwin! How about giving me a hand with some of these uniforms? We'll have to send down the best of those practice pants and trash the rest. We can't get another year out of those and still be decent on the practice field. I think Pruitt will buy us some new ones for the varsity. After all, some parent might complain."

"Ok. I've done about all the sorting I can here, anyway."

After they had finished packing away the game jerseys and pants in the locker and stacked the helmets overhead, Coach Stevens suggested they take a break. Instead of walking back to the coach's office and lying back on the old dusty couch, he cleaned off a stool and Coach Edwin leaned back against a big box full of shoulder pads. This became the first of many conversations about motivation, inspiration, and participation.

"What do you think, Coach Edwin? How do we turn a losing attitude and losing seasons into winning ones?"

"I don't reckon I'd know, Coach. I've never played on a losing team. How about you?"

"Well, yeah. We always lost a few games. Sometimes we lost a lot. I can't remember many losing seasons, though." Coach Stevens was scratching his head and thinking back. He had been a Green Wave. He had never played for his dad, and his game had been mostly basketball, but he couldn't exactly remember a losing season.

"My school won a state basketball championship back in the fifties. Our school was so small we didn't play much competition in football. We won our share in the district and even beat the county rivalry once, and they were twice the size of our school and in double-A.", said Edwin.

"Well, one thing is for certain. We can't develop a winning tradition without participation. Got any suggestions on how we get most of the boys out and to stay out though the varsity years?" Stevens kicked a loose helmet over into the corner.

"I just remember how crazy it was at my high school the year the Green Dragons won the State Championship in basketball. The players got more attention than the mayor in the county seat. There were a lot of school announcements posted and articles out of newspapers on a large bulletin board. Some coaches wouldn't worry about it, Coach. They think if they want to play, they'll show up. If they don't, we would just be wasting our time, anyhow. We need some of the better athletes that don't come out. Maybe we could talk to them, but maybe it won't do a lot of good in the long run."

Coach Stevens shook his head. "That has always been my attitude. I don't remember my dad ever having to recruit, but this might be different. What do you say about us coming up with a plan to recruit and recognize players? Maybe take this year's squad to the State All-Star game this summer at the coach's clinic?"

quit.

"They deserve something. Especially those sophomores who took a beating and never quit."

"And let's divide up all the 10th through 12th grade boys that we want to come out. Each coach will have a one-on-one talk with his group. I'll see if Pruitt will let us have a meeting during the last class period sometime this spring and we'll talk up our program. Every boy in school will come to the meeting, if, for no other reason, just to get out of class. We'll invite every boy to play Spartan football. Nobody will be turned down." Stevens was on a roll.

"You could end up with a lot of dead weight out there."

"Maybe." Coach Stevens was wondering if dead weight might not be better than no weight at all.

"Reckon we could get a Booster Clubgoing with the parents, Coach?"

Stevens looked at Coach Edwin. He smiled as he felt the plan begin to come together.

"I'll check with Pruitt on that, too. Maybe we could get organized this spring and have things rolling by the time the season gets started."

The rest of the equipment was forgotten. The next couple of hours were spent in the overcrowded closet with Edwin making a big dent in the shoulder pad box, as the two coaches made no attempt to reign in their enthusiasm. A weekly bulletin board with news and game pictures, an end-of-two-a-days buffet for players and parents, and a wall of fame for all-district or better players were planned. The sweat coming off the coaches was not entirely due to the stuffy equipment room.

Buzz heard all about it from Jesse. The old man was all in a tizzy when he got back from the meeting. Pruitt had called an organizational meeting for a Boosters Club. Coach Stevens had sent home an invitation to all parents by the boys who showed up for his meeting during the last period of the last day before exams. He had been right in the turnout. Almost every boy took the opportunity to get out of class and he had to move the meeting from the PE classroom to the auditorium. Buzz had brought two invitations home. One for his mother and one for Jesse. Jesse was the only one that had the time or interest.

"He called the group 'The Athletic Supporters'. Broke everybody up. After the laughing died down, Pruitt split us up into groups to do some brainstorming. Then we got back together, and you wouldn't believe the suggestions that came out of such a small group. He wrote them all down on a blackboard. You could see the pride in some faces as their idea got written up."

"What did you recommend, Jesse?" Buzz asked.

"Don't matter. It got written up, too. But, when it was all agreed to, only two was moved to the top of the list."

"What were they?" Buzz was getting a little impatience with Jesse.

"Pat the players on the back no matter where you saw them or what the score was."

"And the other?"

"Be there. At the game. At the gate when the players come on the field. At the locker room when they come out after a game. We're gonna be part of the team, Buzz. As much as you, or the students, or the coaches. We've got a part to play, too."

"Don't see how you have much to do with winning a game unless you put on the pads and carry the ball." Buzz had hoped for something more.

"Coach Stevens doesn't see it that way. The way he explained it, there are a lot of ingredients that make up a winner. Sometimes it's more than the score on the board."

"The only winners I've ever seen had more points than the other team."

"You're young, Son. Us older guys knew what he was talking about. Pride is a powerful thing."

Buzz didn't think any more about it. He had moved up to Varsity at the end of the JV season and actually got into a couple of games for a play or two. It hadn't made any difference. They still lost the game. Now he was hoping for a better season coming up. He was a sophomore and his brother Grogan a junior and they had a few seniors coming back. Buzz spent most of the summer at the ball field playing touch and at the slab taking abusive comments from Patrick about the Spartan football team. He shrugged it all off. He was pretty much the dominant player on the slab now and Patrick didn't get a lot of endorsements. In a few days practice would start and he would have less time for the slab, or Patrick.

8

RED BANDANA

Two-a-days started. Buzz was surprised with the turnout. About thirty guys showed up for the varsity, and about twenty of them were decent athletes. When he looked around, he couldn't name a one that hadn't returned from the JV team. This was a switch. With the extra bodies, there would be no problem running the first team as a unit, both on offense and defense.

The only disappointment to Buzz was that Coach wouldn't let him play defense. He still got his pop into a guy once in a while, especially when he found one standing around daydreaming. Coach Michaels had taught him back in Little League that you needed to pay attention even if you weren't on the first team.

What really surprised Buzz was the meal served up to celebrate the end of two-a-day practices. He had never seen so much food. Every Spartan mom, or Booster mom, or just moms, had brought at least one dish. Some had made two or three. Coaches Stevens, Lowery, Kirby, and Edwin were invited to the head of the line, but the coaches declined. They said it was the players who had done the hard work and sweated out in that August sun and they would be the first in line. Buzz didn't have to be asked twice. He jumped in line, elbowing for position with the rest of the players.

When the meal was over, Coach Stevens introduced the varsity and had the eighth-grade and JV team to stand up. He showed a little of the last scrimmage game on the video and ran a few plays in slow motion so the Booster s (they quit calling themselves the Athletic Supporters) could watch the single-wing's deception. Most everybody lost the ball at full speed. So did the defense, Buzz thought.

That would not be the only surprise for Buzz. The school seemed to have done a complete flip. Spirit. Something Buzz had only heard about but never seen at Giles High School. A big bulletin board in the middle of the lower hall had all the preseason news articles and predictions by *The Roanoke Times* as to the district leaders. There were pictures of most of the players in the single wing formation or running a play. A big banner across the top read 'Play Spartan Football'.

Buzz was impressed. Evidently, most of the school was, too. Each morning a group gathered around, reading the articles or pointing at pictures. Some were players, and some were friends of players, and some wished they were players. Even Patrick had been spotted at the board. Probably making fun, but still there and giving notice.

Someone had posted a poem, or song, on the board. Buzz read it:

GILES SPARTANS

SITTING ON A HILL TOP, NEAR
ANGELS REST,

STANDS GILES HIGH SCHOOL,
CLASS DOUBLE A'S BEST.

PROUDLY, WE WAVE OUR FLAG,
RED AND WHITE.

FLOYD COUNTY BUFFALOES ARE IN
FOR A FIGHT.

SPARTANS - GILES HIGH SPARTANS!

THE CLASS OF THE DOUBLE A
SCHOOLS.

SPARTANS - GILES HIGH SPARTANS!

THIS YEAR THE SINGLE-WING
RULES.

That afternoon, the choir had picked out
the tune and was singing it in class. The rest

of the week you could hear it being hummed by a couple of girls strolling down the hall, just a step or two in front of a couple of boys trailing behind and mocking with their version of the song.

Buzz was enjoying school more this year. It wasn't just the football team winning their first game and beating the Buffaloes 46-0. But he felt closer to his teammates, and there seemed to be excitement in the hallways before classes, at lunch, and between classes when a group got together. He wasn't sure about during class when the teacher's excitement meant more work and higher expectations. There appeared to be a real positive feeling and spirit of cooperation among the whole student body. The troublemakers were finding it hard to find someone to argue a point or even stay around long enough to listen to their opinion. More and more, they became less and less.

"Hey, Buzz. Looking at your picture on the board, are you?"

"More than one, Patrick."

"Gotta give you credit, Buzz. You ran good against Floyd. Must have gained fifty yards or more." Patrick elbowed his buddy Anthony.

"More than a hundred, Patrick. A hundred and forty-seven, to be exact. Could be looking at your mug up here, you know."

"Not me, Man. I'd have to punch out Stevens if he ever got in my face like he does you all. Besides, half of them sissies will quit after Narrows kicks your butt Friday night. Heard my old man say that the men at the plant are talking about their Green Wave ripping that bandana off your head and sticking it down your pants."

"I got another one, Patrick. Those slow lizards down there have to tackle me first, you know."

Buzz walked up the hall and left Patrick and Anthony to ribbing each other. It did rankle his craw a little that talk might be starting about the bandana. It was part of his uniform now. Taking it off just to avoid a threat might bring bad luck. He'd just wait and see if the coach said anything.

Coach Stevens did. That evening was to be their last day of full contact for the week, and Coach had just finished with the pep talk that he always gave to start a practice. All week the pre-practice talk had been about the mistakes made in the Floyd game and what they would do in this practice to correct them.

Today, the focus was on what to expect from Narrows and the adjustments to be made to defend them. The team listened to their individual instructions and how all of it would come together as a team. The coaches spent hours going over the film of the opponent for the upcoming game. Each player had to learn who lined up across from him, and his defensive responsibility. It was all part of knowing what to do before they got on the practice field to learn how to do it.

"Ok, Men. Let's put it together here." Coach held out his right hand.

As a group they all came together in a huddle and placed their hands one on top of another. Coach would have one final word.

"Men, I got wind of a rumor today, and it may well be just that, a rumor. A friend of mine who works down at Celco said he overheard talk about trouble Friday night at the game. Now, I don't put much stock in athletes playing dirty or getting personal on the field, and I'm sure the same goes for the coach down at Narrows. It seems there is some jealousy in the plant about Buzz's success this year and some of them think his wearing the bandana is a way of showing off, or being different. Now, we know better. He's worn that thing ever since I have seen him play football, from Little League on up. Now I don't know if it is his badge, or symbol, or what. All I know is, I respect his right, and it's not against the rules. Friday night, I'll have a red bandana tied in my belt loop, and if any of you want to wear one you won't get any objection from me. If they want to rip off a bandana, we'll give them more than they can carry back down the river. Now, we got practice to finish, and I don't want to hear any more about it. Ready! Go!"

Nothing else was said. Buzz was embarrassed. He kept waiting for some comment or other. The only thing he noticed was the level of intensity had picked up a lot. The holes closed faster. The receivers couldn't get open. No smiles.

That night Grogan told his mom what happened. Buzz could have killed him.

"They wouldn't deliberately hurt him, would they, Grogan?"

"Naw. Just talk, Mom. A bunch of guys trying to stir up a little rivalry."

"Well, they might just stir up more than they can chew. I'm going to that game, and I'll wear a red bandana in my hair, and one around my neck, and maybe one or two wrapped around my fist. If they lay a finger on Buzz, I'll ...."

"Come on, Mom! They are supposed to lay a finger on me. In fact, they are supposed to take my head off, if they can. Grogan, see what you have started?"

Buzz stomped out of the kitchen and headed down to the slab. This was crazy. His mom had never been to a game in her life. He had wanted her to, but not now, not for this reason. Maybe by game time Friday night, it would all die down.

Friday night came. The game was on the Spartan's home field. Buzz and the rest of the team were sequestered in the Ag building, as was customary for a home game. They had dressed in the Varsity locker room and walked over to sit down in the long hallway where a lot of them took shop classes. No talking. No smiles. Coach Stevens had set the precedent his first year as coach. He wanted the players thinking about the game. The dressing procedure reminded Buzz of a church choir that entered the chapel with little expression on their faces, marched to their seats (the same one every Sunday), serious thoughts, and little life until they raised the roof top with bellowing voices. He had his seat on the bench in the dressing room as well as his spot on the floor in the hall. An assistant coach was always available if a player or manager needed help in remembering what tonight was all about.

Buzz broke his routine tonight. Twice he had to get up and rush to the toilet to throw up nothing but heaving gasps. He was nervous. Not afraid, just nervous, and he didn't know why. He seldom got jittery over a game. He had thought about the bandana and had waited to the last minute before he finally put it on. The superstition, if that was what it was, was more fearful than all the

Green Wave put together. It was no big deal. He walked back and took his spot in the hall.

Jesse saw that it was a big deal. He had heard about the bandanna escapade from Shakey, who had heard it from the men at the café, who had heard it at the plant. He got to the game early, as usual. He brought Buzz's mom, which had been a big shock in itself. What he saw when he walked through the gate was almost more than his old ticker could take. There were hundreds, no thousands, of people in the stands. Green and gold on the visitor's side and nothing but red in the Spartan stands. A group of men were standing on the hill to the right of the home side. They later became known as 'The Hill Gang'.

Someone with a red Spartan jacket on and a red bandana tied around his neck ran out on the field and spiked a stick with a red bandana flag on it into the ground. A roar went up from the Giles stands. A minute later, a young man with a green jacket ripped a pennant with a large green 'N' on a gold background from the hands of a startled Green

Wave cheerleader and dashed out to the middle of the field and spiked it into the ground. A loud cheer sprung forth from the visitor's side of the field.

Jesse just stood inside the gate and looked around. Everyone had on a red bandana. He knew that Buzz's mom had made a fuss about wearing one, and he had finally given in and tied one through the belt loop in his pants. But, he would have never imagined this. He eased on around the track to find a seat and bumped into Patrick and Anthony leaving the concession with a Coke in each hand. To be spiked with something a little stronger, thought Jesse. He could easily ignore Patrick and his crew, but this time he turned around to take another look. Patrick had tied a red bandana around his head the way Buzz wore his and had two more tied to his waist. Jesse felt his mouth spring open.

"Catching flies, Jesse?" Patrick smiled.

Jesse just stared.

"Don't expect them to beat the Green Wave. Just had to support Buzz. Ought to be fun tonight, don't you think, Jesse?"

"Reckon so, Patrick. Don't you start something. We got a good thing going, and, if I see you stirring up trouble, I'll call the cops myself."

"No worry, Jesse." Patrick and Anthony hurried on to join the group on the hill.

Jesse hurried on to find a seat next to Shakey. Buzz's mom would have to fend for herself at a football game. There were some traditions, or habits, you just didn't break. Anyhow, analyzing the game with Shakey was fun this year. They had learned enough about the single-wing to give lessons to Red Grange, the 'Galloping Ghost', of the University of Illinois, if he were still around. Between watching most practices, every game, and the game film at the Booster 's meeting, they had become pretty much experts.

They had not only learned the formations, but had learned the plays by the number call given by Coach Stevens in practice. Thirty-eight meant the blocking back would pivot, receive a fake handoff from the fullback, with his hands in his crotch, palms up and forearms against his hip bones. He would fake a pitch to the tailback, sweep around the right end in the two-hole and continue through the four-hole and pick up a block on the first man to his outside. The wingback would glance off the defensive end and go down field and block the halfback. The fullback would take a six-inch side step from his crouched stance as he received the ball, palms up with hands near his crotch, extend the ball to the blocking-back and withdraw it as he covered it with both arms, and run through the hole provided by the double-team block of the guard and right tackle, and the trap of the left tackle.

The whole thing was poetry in motion. No one would know where the ball was, especially the defensive linebackers. The defensive lineman wouldn't stand a chance. Even the big studs couldn't hold off a double team, and they never knew where the trap was coming from. The hole would be there. If the blocks were successful on the linebackers, or the deception was good by the single-wing backs, you could count on a nice gain.

Sometimes Jesse explained the play to Shakey, and sometimes Shakey had the honors. Either way, they didn't have time, or inclinations, to waste their new-found knowledge on women or kids. It had to be appreciated.

The game didn't start well nor end well. Jesse watched Buzz fumble the opening kickoff. He must be nervous because Buzz had the best hands on the team. This was the first time Coach had played him on special teams. Giles went into halftime down 21-0. The Green Wave were looking good, and they also were undefeated after two games into the season. Patrick might throw in the towel, but Shakey and Jesse would hang in there with the team until the last second ticked off the clock.

It did, and Narrows won the game 28-13. It was not the 48-0 beating they had dished out to the Spartans the year before, but the same nauseating feeling to Jesse and the new Spartan hopefuls. Jesse and Shakey kept their seats long after the throng had filed out of the stadium.

"Reckon the spark has died, Jesse?" Shakey held his head, cupped in hands that were supported by his elbows propped on his knees, with his feet replacing the seat of a departed fan on the bleacher in front of them.

"I don't think so, Shakey. Let's just hope it's round one we lost. We'll fix up our wounds, and come back more determined than ever."

"Come on, Jesse!" Buzz's mother was hollering at him from down near the fence.

"You go on, Patricia. Shakey and I have to get some hotdogs at the concession stand and take to the locker room. I'll meet you at the car in about thirty minutes. It's unlocked."

"Well, you hurry up. This night air has got a chill to it. You know I have to get up early in the morning to go to work."

"We won't be long, Patricia."

She walked away and Jesse and Shakey stepped over the bleacher seats on their way to get the hotdogs.

"I guess that will be her one and only game, huh, Jesse?"

"I don't know, Shakey. She usually just works and cleans after those kids. She sure was excited about tonight. Or mad. I guess everybody will forget about those bandanas now that nothing happened. I wonder if Ralph just made that up about the talk at the plant and Green Wave fans stealing Buzz's bandana. Well, Patricia's got several to wipe the sweat with next summer when she's working the garden."

9

SCHOOL SPIRIT

Buzz's mom never missed another game, and she always wore a red bandana. Thousands of other Spartan fans did the same. Two games later, a caravan eased down Interstate 81 with red bandanas flying from radio antennas and flapping from rolled-up windows. The Spartans had bounced back and tied the Blacksburg Indians 6-6, and spirits were high as they headed to Wytheville. The spark didn't die, but burst forth into a roaring fire.

Last week the Indians had arrived at Spartan field to find a full stadium with huge red bandana flags surrounding the top of the home-side bleachers. A new sign was in place over the concession stand. The now 'Bandana Bar' was selling out of food and drink before the third quarter was over. 'Bandanamania' had swept through central and eastern Giles County. Win or lose, home or away, the Spartan faithful now always outnumbered the opposing fans.

Coach Stevens bought a couple of dozen red Spartan jackets out of his equipment fund to see if they would sell. In three days he had to reorder. Students and fans alike, who wouldn't have been seen dead in Giles colors, were now grabbing up everything with "Giles" or "Spartan" written on it. The shoe store had stocked bolts of red bandana cloth to make flags or scarves. The town of Pearisburg looked like a Fourth of July celebration every Friday. Hundreds of bandana flags were hung on every block and in front of most stores or offices. Driving down Route 460 or 100 you could see a flag or a Spartan head stuck in the front yard of dedicated, or maybe fanatic, fans. Fridays also became bandana day at Giles High School. The Pep Club sponsored shirt days and hat days, but Fridays were reserved for bandana day.

The excitement at the school had affected everyone, it seemed. Every Friday morning, for the last half of the season, the PA announcement began with a mixed group of boys and girls singing the song someone had posted on the bulletin board.

LET'S ALL GO

LET'S ALL GO O O O, OUT TO SEE THE SPARTANS.

LET'S ALL GO O O O, OUT TO SEE THE SPARTANS.

WE'LL GRAB A SLAW-BURGER, FRIES, AND A BOTTLE OF SPRITE

COME ON (BOBCATS), WE'RE READY TO FIGHT.

LET'S ALL GO O O O, OUT TO SEE THE SPARTANS.

LET'S ALL GO O O O, OUT TO SEE THE SPARTANS.

Out they went to see the Spartans in red jackets, t-shirts, sweat suits, and red bandanas. The Spartans went on to an exuberant 6-3-1 regular season. They not only beat the Radford Bobcats 27-0 for the first time in school history, but the shutout was the first for the Bobcats on their home turf.

Buzz, as a sophomore, played in eight of the ten games, carried the ball 172 times, and gained 1010 yards. He read the bulletin board news articles every Monday morning. Sometimes Patrick would meander over and put a hand on his shoulder and point out how many yards Buzz had gained in the Friday night game. Buzz couldn't help but smile when he happened upon Patrick and the dirty red bandana he wore throughout the football season. It had been a good year, but Buzz wasn't satisfied. The Spartans had barely finished with a winning record, and that had been done before.

10

COMMUNITY PRIDE

During the winter season, Buzz and a few other football players helped the coaches move the weight room to the basement of the high school. They cleaned out the utility room, put down carpet leftovers donated by a local carpet dealer, hung some odd-shaped mirrors, and posted achievement charts on a board. Starting this year, the weight room would be open Monday, Wednesday, and Friday after school. Coach Stevens also taught a weight-lifting class for anyone interested. Buzz had already given up on basketball and dedicated his off-season to getting bigger, faster, and stronger.

The excitement died down a little after football season, but school spirit seemed to be there to stay. The school shirts and jackets were part of the everyday dress for most of the student body. The basketball crowds were a little larger and noisier. The student absentee rate was down. Spartan pride was bubbling forth like a volcano struggling to erupt, both in school and out.

Jesse went to the cafe with Shakey a couple of times a month. They still took a lot of static from the Narrows fans, but now they talked of what was coming next year. The bets were covered well before the season started. Jesse now wore a red bandana tied around his neck like the cowboys used to wear. Shakey wore one of the Spartan jackets that Coach had first sold. He was superstitious and refused to wash it until Giles beat Narrows. Jesse was optimistic about next season, but he also knew that Narrows had a lot on their side. Narrows had tradition. Giles just had a fever. He might not want to sit next to Shakey by the time the third game of the season came around.

The cafe was not the only thing buzzing. Celco, the big factory on the edge of

New River, was appropriately located halfway between the two rivals. The employees came from all parts of the county and the loyalty was pretty well divided between the schools. Management had never noticed much in the way of competition among the employees before the past year. They had come to work, talked about hunting or fishing or the weather, and dashed for the parking lot as soon as their shift was over.

Now they arrived early enough to overlap the previous shift, lounged around in the parking lot, took extra minutes for their breaks, packed the cafeteria even if they brought their lunch, and hung around the lot long after they should have been home. Single-wing football was a hot topic. Even though the Green Wave fans wouldn't give an inch on who was best, they enjoyed reliving the days of the single-wing and the tradition left them by The Coach. Shakey and Ralph always attracted a crowd as they drew out formations on a dusty table top. Thirty-two buck was the favorite play for the Spartan fans. Jesse had to laugh when Shakey told him about drawing it up on the stall door in the men's room and labeling it as 'The Green

Wave Slayer'. Top management wasn't complaining. Sick leave was almost non-existent.

A new decade was just beginning for young Coach Stevens. He had taken an old offense he had learned from his father and implemented it at Giles High School the very first year he became head football coach. This would be the fourth year and he only had one winning season, just barely. It was a fun offense, and something that had generated spirit, excitement, and pride at Giles this past year.

He still wasn't sure if he should stick with it. Nobody else in the state was running the Single-Wing. It had practically disappeared with the I-formation and pro-set taking its place. If he did stick with the ancient offense and had a couple more losing seasons, he might find himself out of a head coaching job. If he couldn't run the Single-Wing, would he want to coach football? He loved it.

The players were mastering the formation and deception. He had more players out for varsity last year than there had been for all three levels in the past ten or twenty years. It surely wasn't his good looks or pleasant demeanor that brought out the majority of athletes at Giles. The student body and fans were equally excited about something the team was doing. It had to be the Single-Wing. He had little choice anyhow. He couldn't, or wouldn't, coach anything else.

Coach Stevens and his two varsity assistants went to the coaching clinic held during the summer at UVA. It was a good opportunity to pick up techniques and pick the brains of other coaches in the state. No one asked about the Single-Wing offense, and they didn't bring it up. He only knew the coaches that he had played against the past couple of years. One of those, Coach Norman, was getting plenty of attention. Not only was he the main speaker at a couple of sessions, but he always had a group of coaches surrounding him during breaks and at lunch. Norman deserved the attention. He had been around several years and had been successful. Coach

Stevens recalled the whipping Norman had laid on the Spartans the last few years.

The clinic proved more beneficial for the time Coach Stevens and his assistants had to go over plans for the upcoming season. It was this trip that made forty-four their bread-and-butter play. It was a quick, smack in the mouth, power play. Against a six-man defensive line, and the Single-Wing saw a lot of that, the blocking-back would trap the first man, head up to outside the wingback. The wingback would double-team with the tight end the first man inside. The fullback would run three steps parallel to the line of scrimmage, cut off the blocking-back's trap, go through the hole and block the first man to outside. The tailback would take the direct snap from center, run three steps parallel to the line of scrimmage, and arc into the four-hole right on the fullback's tail. The seven-man would block head up to inside. The eight-man would key the defensive strong side line-backer and if he fires, step up and seal him at the line, or pull and meet him on the inside of the four-hole. The nine-man and center would block head up or inside and the left end and ten-man would block down field on the offside linebacker and safety.

"Coach, I believe we need to concentrate on a variety of plays to keep them confused. Deception is the key to our offense." Coach Edwin was shaking his head.

"I disagree, Coach. Deception is part of our offense. Power blocking with double teams and traps is our strength. We could tell them we're coming through the four-hole and they couldn't stop us short of a five-yard gain. Plus, it's quick. They have no time to adjust." Coach Stevens replied with determination.

He pulled out a new sheet on the legal pad and drew out the play forty-four:

"Ok, Coach. I agree that would be difficult to stop. Let's don't forget to mix it up a little to keep them off balance." Edwin knew who the boss was.

"Don't worry. Bread and butter don't mean we won't throw in a lot of jam. I agree with you, too. We gotta have some variety, but I want a play that we are comfortable with. I have confidence in forty-four."

They left the clinic after the All-Star football game. A few of the boys from the region had made the team, but only one Spartan. Giles had won only six games, but that was good enough to get Curtis recognized as one of the best safeties in the state. Without Curtis, it might not have been six wins. Coach Stevens started his Wall of Fame with one picture.

Buzz and his brother Grogan, who was now driving the old '72 Chevy pickup, picked up Gordon Matney, and met Mace, Carl, Cecil, and several more of the players out behind the tennis courts at school for a little pickup game of touch. They were getting anxious for the season to start and tired of the summer dragging on. It wouldn't do to let the teachers know they were ready for school. Not ready for classes, just school and football.

After a couple of hours of sweating and running after bomb passes from Steve Charles, they decided to go sit on the steps and watch the cheerleaders practice. Buzz thought they put in an awful lot of hours just to stand on the sidelines and yell. He couldn't figure out why they needed to start in early summer, go to camps, and practice two hours after school every day to do no more than they did. Why, the team only had twenty days of practice before the first game!

The girls were working on a dance routine under the direction of their sponsor, Ms. Farrier. They were trying to match up the steps to a song they had written and Buzz had to admit it was pretty catchy. Brandi, Pam, and Rachel were leading, and Ruth, Lottie, and the rest of the girls were tracing their steps. Ms. Farrier would stop them every few steps and make them repeat in slow motion. Buzz could see the sweat rolling off their brows and realized the boys had not put out any more effort out there chasing each other and the ball. He especially liked the song:

SPARTAN FEVER

by Pam – and the cheerleaders

*I was easin' down on Spartan ground,
when my temperature started to rise.*

*Well, I was workin' up a sweat, but it
weren't for the heat - much to my surprise.*

*Yeah, all of Giles was feelin' it, too. The
reason was simple and clear.*

*You see the Spartans are gonna tear 'em
up. It's really gonna happen this year.*

Cause we've got - SPARTAN FEVER

*The kind that has no cure. Yeah! It's
Spartan fever*

Gonna blow 'em out for sure!

Well, some are big and some are small, but there's somethin' different about them all.

They're mean, ah, man - they're bad. They're gonna say bad things about your coaches.

The Bandana Bandits have just begun, and this year the Spartans are Number One!

We'll beat the Celtics and the Knights. Those fighting Blues won't even fight.

We'll scalp the Indians and the Cats, beat the Waves so bad they'll never come back.

We'll roll all over the Demons and whip the Maroons, too,

We'll wipe up the Tide and Cavaliers, Nothing Grundy or Falcons can do

'cept bow to the red and blue.

Cause we've got - SPARTAN FEVER

The kind that has no cure. Yeah! It's Spartan fever

Gonna blow 'em out for sure!

The fever's bad and we are cool, but what's so different about this school?

We've got a winner that'll blow their wits when they get a taste of our quick blitz.

'Cause way down here in the land of Spartan. All past seasons are forgotten.

Look ahead, look ahead, look ahead

State title!!!

Ooo-who??? Can you believe it????

This Spartan Fever is sweeter than wine, with State title runnin' up my spine.

We'll always beat the other nerds. Hey, World, have you heard the word?

They're mean - I mean they're bad. They'll bite your foot.

I mean they're gonna hurt ya, baby. We'll have the best darn season we've ever had!!

- *SPARTAN FEVER*

The kind that has no cure. Hey! Spartan fever

Gonna blow 'em out for sure!

We've got - SPARTAN FEVER

The kind that has no cure. Yeah! It's Spartan fever

Gonna blow 'em out for sure!

Buzz and the group stood up and gave them a standing ovation. The girls blushed and turned their backs. Ms. Farrier asked them to leave and they did.

"I like that song." Grogan said as he and Matney were trying to sing it.

"Yeah, if it was only true." Buzz replied without trying to join in. It looked to him like the cheerleaders were opening their mouths and inserting their big feet. Until they beat somebody, they should keep it quiet and take one game at a time.

11

ATHLETIC SUPPORTERS

The next month, the 10th of August, two-a-days started. It was the biggest turn out for the Varsity and JV teams in school history. The Eighth- Grade wouldn't start for another two weeks. Grogan and Carl were elected team captains. Buzz picked out his seat and dressing station near the support column where he could rest his back after a hard day's practice. He had sat there last year and found it supported more than the ceiling. Everyone seemed to reclaim the station he had last year, and the newcomers filled in wherever they could. Some of the beginners dressed in the shower stall. Buzz noticed a couple of bandanas tied to blue jeans, but nobody else wore one under his helmet during practice.

Two-a-day practices ended just before school started. The Booster Club and parents brought in dishes of food for a pot-luck dinner in celebration of the end of the practices and the beginning of the regular season. Buzz loved the dinners and he always ate more than he should and always paid for it the night after.

Coach Stevens, as always, sounded a word of caution. He announced to the crowd that "we have a bunch of hard-working men, but I don't know if we can win a ballgame, yet. I do expect every game to be a battle, and I don't think you will find a Spartan in this room to lie down and quit. We're not big, but we're tough. The other team will know they have been in a fight when the game's over."

Coach Stevens talked on. He wasn't a speaker by nature, or by choice, but he liked to leave the team feeling good at the end of a hard day's practice, and he wanted to leave the faithful Spartan fans feeling good and appreciated.

"The Spartans of Ancient Greece would be proud of those here at Giles High School. Not just these players who are well above the average, but the great fans who have let the whole New River District know that we are here. Spartan fever has truly set in. The spirit and enthusiasm developed over the past couple of years has infected us all. To see thousands of you fans show up at a game not only gives these guys the recognition they deserve, but it fills us all with inspiration. Those of us that can't claim to be a Spartan by birthright can claim to be so by association. Spartan pride is alive at Giles High School. I thank YOU!"

The thunderous applause made Buzz feel good. More so than the food that was now cramping his stomach. He wondered if most of the other guys felt the way he did. He would play Spartan football even if he sat on the bench or shagged footballs for the punter. The next week would be a long one. But Friday night would surely come and so would the Fighting Blues. He would be ready.

Monday's practice proved to be the start of serious business. Buzz could tell by the look in Coach's eyes that nothing less than perfect would do. The backs did extra repetitions of each play. If Coach Stevens could detect the ball during the exchange between the fullback and blocking-back, then they did the play again. Several times he would demonstrate the hand-off in slow motion. The double teams did some extra blocking. If they couldn't drive the block off the line, then they were expected to bury him where he was. Grogan would be the first back through the hole with Buzz close on his tail. If Coach Stevens called thirty-two buck lateral, Spencer would pull from the eight-man position and lead the sweep around the right end. If a back on the practice squad was bold enough to take him on, Don would plow over him like a horse through new ground. Most of the time Buzz watched as they ran around his lead blocker, and he easily cut the other way. Often, he carried the ball the length of the field, or until the whistle sounded.

Two-a-days were over, but the Monday through Wednesday practices continued to be tough. Two and a half hours on the field going full steam and sometimes another half-an-hour in the film room watching and re-watching mistakes they made.

Coach Stevens didn't hesitate to slow the film down and call out a name.

"Cecil, you block with your shoulder pads, not with your hips. How are you going to sustain that block and drive him down the field by turning sideways?"

"Benny, if he falls down, roll him. Keep your feet moving and get him out of the hole. We've got to have somewhere to run the ball. We can't do that with you and your "friend" hugging each other right in the middle of the hole. Get him out of there!"

"Steve, you ought to buy a ticket. If you're going to watch the ball carrier then you should find a seat in the stands and be a spectator. Watch this guy you bumped. After you stopped and turned around to watch the ball, he recovered and made the tackle on Grogan. We picked up three yards when maybe we could've scored."

Coach Stevens not only filmed the games on Friday night, but he was probably the only coach in the district that filmed his practice sessions. Coach Lowery would often take the linemen in to watch a film while the specialty teams worked out before the full practice began. Sometimes Coach Stevens would keep the backs and ends a few minutes after practice and analyze the day's work. He believed you fixed mistakes by bringing them to the front.

Buzz was glad when Thursday rolled around. The team had spent an extra thirty minutes at the end of practice on Wednesday putting pads into their new game pants and scrubbing their helmets. Someone had given Coach Stevens a computer graphic design of a football with a single wing attached to one side. He had passed it on to a sales representative who returned with a small transparent decal that had a red football with a "G" between the laces and sprouting a single wing. Coach had decided that each player would paste a red single wing football decal above each ear hole on their helmet. Buzz loved it. Not only were they the Spartans, they were the Single-Wing Spartans.

The pre-game practice was short. They walked through every play and formation that the scouts had brought back, or that had seen on film, of the Fighting Blues. Buzz hated to see the new red jerseys and shiny helmets get messed up, but Coach Stevens wanted the new wore off before game time. Every player was expected to have a scratch or two on his helmet and grass stains or dirt on his uniform by the end of practice on Thursday. Coach didn't want them standing around on Friday night looking at how pretty they were. He told them about the new pickup truck he had bought a couple of years ago.

"It was a pretty thing. Bright red with white racing stripes down the side. For two days, I wouldn't take it out of the drive way. When I finally drove it to town and back, I washed it and buffed it down with a soft cloth. My wife had to clean off her shoes before she got in and wipe her fingerprints off the door handle when she got out. I had the sharpest wheels in Giles County, and it was going to stay that way. For two weeks, that pickup was never on a dirt road.

"Well, look at it now. It gets washed maybe twice a year if it doesn't rain. It's got stuff I need in the bed, under the seat, behind the seat, and in the floor. My wife drives it any time she wants. I've had that truck everywhere. Down on the river, up on the mountain, and even a few trips to the landfill.

"Yeah, two days after that dumb neighbor kid ran his bicycle into my new truck and put a scratch all the way down the driver's side, I took it through every mud hole in Bailey's Gap.

"Now, get out there and get the new off! Tomorrow night we have a battle with the Fighting Blues, and I want you and those shiny helmets to look like you were in a war."

All of the Spartans had a smile on their faces. Buzz also had a twinge running up his spine. He wondered how many of the others couldn't wait for tomorrow night.

Buzz and Grogan rode home with Dalton and Matney. They were unusually quiet. Each was thinking about the first game of the season and their responsibility. It was going to be the first game of 1980. A new decade. Buzz wondered if that meant anything. Would it be a new beginning for

Giles High School? Or would they lose all the momentum they had gained last year and drift back to where they had always been? If they could win just one more game than last year, could it be the beginning of a tradition?

When they got home, Buzz and Grogan found a message on the table that their mother would be working over a shift down at the store. The relief girl had called in sick. Would they heat up food out of the fridge and make sure Allison was home before they went to bed, and be sure to do their homework?

Grogan set the food out on the table, filled his plate, and stuck it in the microwave. Both of them were starved. Buzz would have to fix his own. He finished off the bowl of leftover fried potatoes and filled the rest of his plate with brown beans and a slab of cornbread. He didn't bother with the microwave. If Allison hadn't eaten, she would have to make do with a sandwich. She should have been home anyhow. Their mother could use a little help, and he and Grogan were pretty wiped out after football practice.

" I'll put away the dishes if you'll call Becky's house and check on Allison." Buzz said, as he washed his plate at the sink.

"OK." Grogan didn't care much for washing dishes, anyhow.

When Buzz finished up, he walked out to the front porch and looked toward the mountains. It would be dark shortly, thanks to daylight savings time. By the end of October they would still be on the practice field when darkness fell. Across the street and down the road about three houses, he could see Jesse sitting in his old wooden rocker. The slow roll back and forth showed Buzz that Jesse was in time with his thinking. Buzz wondered where Shakey was? Usually they got together after supper down at the horseshoe pits or lounged around on each other's porches.

He ambled on down the street and slumped down on the edge of the steps with his back resting against the post supporting the roof.

"How did practice go, Buzz?" Jesse didn't break his rhythm with the rocker.

"Pretty easy day on Thursday. Just a pre-game walk through."

"Are we good enough to beat Parry McCluer?" Jesse pulled out a bag of Redman chewing tobacco and stuffed a fist-full into his jaw.

"Guess we'll find out tomorrow night. We did all right in the scrimmage against Grundy."

"Yeah, better than last year when them and the G-men both kicked our butts all over the field. I don't know if we beat Grundy though. You let that kid catch you when you should've scored on that 60-yard run near the end of the scrimmage."

"Ah, Jesse, I was just checking out his speed. Nobody's going to catch me when I break into the open."

"They will, if you look over your shoulder. Put your sights on the goal line and don't slow down till you've run through the end zone."

"It won't happen again, Jesse. Where's Shakey?"

"Oh, he stopped off at the café. I hope he's just talking up the game. Some of those guys get the wrong kind of spirit. I just wanted to come on home and relax a little. Let my thinking go whichever way the wind wants to blow it. Maybe play the game tonight in my head and have you score a couple of touchdowns."

"Maybe you should save those touchdowns till tomorrow night."

Jesse rocked forward a little farther and spit a stream of brown juice into the dying grass six feet away.

"Maybe. But the time for talking is over with. Time for doing. We just need to win tomorrow night. One step at a time."

"That's what Coach says."

"You guys listen to that young feller. He'll do his job. You just do yours and Grogan do his and all the rest of the players do theirs, and that's all it'll take. Team work. A Single-Wing team is hard to beat."

Jesse's rocker was picking up speed. About every tenth roll he would push up on his toes and spit into the grass.

"You get on home and get your rest. I've got a game to finish tonight."

Buzz smiled as he eased off the steps. "See you, Jesse. I wish I could play all my games sitting in a comfortable rocker."

Jesse grunted and pulled the wad of tobacco out of his jaw and heaved it in Buzz's direction. That boy was still just a kid. But he was also an exceptional running back. This could be a good year.

Buzz didn't get much rest. He tossed and turned. He replayed in his mind every play the Spartans ran. He squeezed the football tighter. The extra pillow that his mother allowed on his bed was tucked tight under his arm. Hot and exhausted, he finally fell off to sleep. The last thing he remembered was thinking he couldn't look back and be caught from behind. He would keep his eyes on the goal line and run like hell.

12

PEP RALLY

The next day at school was no ordinary Friday. There was excitement in the air. Coach had allowed the players to wear their mesh practice jerseys with their number on the back. The JV and eighth-grade coaches had followed suit. Over one hundred boys in little Giles High School were walking the halls dressed in their proudest fashion.

The cheerleaders were not to be outdone. They all wore their uniforms. Each had a red "G" or miniature single-wing football painted on their cheek.

The student body joined in. Nearly 700 students and teachers had worn red. Red shirts. Bandana shirts or ties. Red bandanas stuck out of hip pockets, tied through belt loops, tied around ponytails, or worn as scarves around their necks. A bright red-covered bulletin board at the end of the hall declared the Spartans to be in the "Red Zone". Maybe they were not yet inside the twenty-yard line, but there was little doubt the whole school was driving hard toward their goal.

Coach Stevens and Mr. Pruitt were definitely communicating on the same wavelength. During the early days of the "Athletic Supporters" the principal let it be known that he and the school would be behind any positive effort to build school spirit and pride. When Coach Stevens asked for a pep rally to kick off the season he was given the OK.

Buzz stood in line in the hallway outside the gymnasium. He could hear the cheerleaders yelling and the pep band playing, but he had doubts about a twenty-minute pep rally amounting to much. He thought the players would be better off somewhere quiet and thinking about the game. He didn't like the idea of being paraded out like heroes when they had yet to win a game.

The doors of the gym opened, the cheerleaders formed a tunnel, and a drum-roll began. Coach Stevens had a microphone in his hand and had already fired up the crowd by telling them what great school spirit the Spartans had and how proud he was to see all that "Red" out there. He started the introduction of the players by telling how they were the finest MEN he had ever had the opportunity to be around and how he would be "honored" to go to war with all of them.

The captains went first. All of the players walked quickly through the cheerleader tunnel to a seat in the bleachers on the other side of the gym. Buzz heard a cheer go up as each player walked across the floor. When Coach called his name and number, he lowered his head and entered the tunnel. The roar grew louder. Someone started a chant. "Buzz", "Buzz", "Buzz". It spread through the crowd and the drummer picked up the rhythm. He had to look up. The 700-student body was on their feet, screaming their heads off, and waving red bandanas. Excitement and adrenaline ripped through his body. His arms, with fists clenched, were forced into the air. He gave a ringing high-five to each of his teammates as he found a seat.

For twenty minutes the deafening roar continued. Each player felt the ovation was his. Each cheerleader believed SHE was the force behind it all.

"WE'VE GOT SPIRIT, YES WE DO."

"WE'VE GOT SPIRIT, HOW ABOUT YOU?"

The chants got stronger as each student Spartan tried to win the "Spirit Stick" awarded to the class that was the loudest.

Buzz had been wrong about the pep rally. It certainly was motivating. He couldn't wait for the game to begin. He wanted a piece of the Fighting Blues NOW!

He didn't have long to wait. By 5:30 the fans started arriving at Spartan Field. Rocky Blankenship and his buddy Alvin had begun a tradition last year to be the first Giles fans in line at the ticket booth. Dressed in their Spartan sweat shirts and red bandanas, they found their seats on the 50-yard line on the top row where they had a back rest against the railing. This year they hung a large bandana flag from a twelve foot pole and tied it to the rail. Rocky had brought along his air-horn hooked to a tank of compressed air. This year the Spartans would be heard as well as seen.

Buzz was exhausted when the game was over. Parry McCluer turned out to be an equal match for the Spartans. The Fighting Blues lived up to their tradition and their name. They were still fighting when Giles ran out the clock to end the game. Buzz had carried the ball 32 times and gained 207 yards. His brother Grogan had added another 142 yards, and Giles took their first big step of the season with a squeaker over Parry McCluer. The final score was Giles 16 and Parry McCluer 15.

There was little celebration after the game. Coach Stevens met with the team for a few minutes in the locker room.

"Men, I'm proud of you! That was a good team we played tonight. Maybe we were lucky, but sometimes the harder you work, the luckier you get. Nobody will outwork us during the week, and you deserve the payday come Friday night. Enjoy this one. When you hit the practice field on Monday, I want those chin-straps on tight. We've got James River next week and we want to make sure we are ready. Now, go get those hotdogs."

Members of the Booster Club were waiting outside the locker room door with a hotdog and a drink for each of the players. Rocky, Alvin, Jesse, and dozens of other fans were there to congratulate and pat them on the back. Buzz smiled as he took the treat from Jesse and headed for the car.

"Good game, Buzz. One down and nine to go."

"One down and 13 to go. We're going all the way."

"I wouldn't say a one-point victory is anything to crow about. I say let's take them one-at-a-time, Buzz."

"I know. That's what the coach says. But, Parry McCluer may be the best team we'll face this year. They were better tonight than Narrows or anyone we played last year. I just know if we work our butts off, nobody will be able to stop this Single-Wing offense. Besides, we've got a good defense. They scored twice, but we held them under a hundred yards on the ground."

"Did that pep rally get into your head, Son? I've never heard you talk so much. You sound pretty sure of yourself all of a sudden."

Jesse's shirt was about to burst with pride. It was about time the kids developed a little self-confidence. He wasn't worried. Coach Stevens would make sure their feet were back on the ground come Monday.

It was more like crashing to the ground. The team sat through thirty minutes of film as Coach Stevens pointed out mistake after mistake.

"We turned the ball over four times. We had nine penalties for a total of 65 yards. We had five drives stopped because of turnovers or penalties. You don't win ball games making mistakes like this. I figure we were plain lucky Friday night.

"Gordon, just because it's a reverse doesn't mean you have to run it out of bounds. Have you ever seen a cut-back?

"Grogan, you lead Buzz through the hole. You're not supposed to help the defense and slow him down. How about getting your tail out of there!

"And, Buzz! My grandmother could break some of those tackles that brought you down. Can't you keep those skinny legs of your pumping? This ain't tough football."

Coach Stevens got on the players that had played the best the worst. They would take it and would make themselves better. The best time for criticism was after a win.

"OK. The way I count it, four turnovers and nine penalties add up to an extra 13 on the hill. Let's see if we can get a little better this week. Let's go!"

Buzz ran the hill at top speed. Most of the players, especially the linemen, hated it. The HILL was a twenty-yard bank on the East end of the practice field that went straight up. It was so steep that some of the 200-pound-plus players ended up walking or crawling the last few yards. The regular routine, Monday through Wednesday was five on the hill. Today it was 18. Friday night the penalties and turnovers would be less.

13

REAL SPARTANS

Friday night they traveled to James River after another great week of school spirit and a send-off pep rally. Two school buses of Spartan players, another for the pep band, a van full of cheerleaders, and several hundred vehicles filled with Giles fans caravanned up I-81 to James River High School.

All the starting offensive and defensive players were on the lead bus with Coach Stevens and the varsity assistant coaches. The rest of the team and managers rode the second bus with the JV coaches that helped out with the game on Friday nights. The eighth-grade coaches were scouting Narrows for next week's game.

Buzz laid his head back on the seat and began thinking about the game. It was Coach Stevens' policy. There would be no talking or horsing around on the way to a game. This was the time for each player to think about his responsibilities during the game. Buzz ran every play in the play book through his mind. Grogan and some of the others that went both ways had the offense and defense to pre-play. Coach Stevens planned the game and his pre-game speech. His halftime remarks would depend on the first half. G.C., the bus driver, tried to stay awake. He would enjoy the ride home a lot better – if the Spartans won.

They did. The final score - Giles 35, James River 7. The second team got to play the fourth quarter and only gave up one touchdown. In three quarters of a game, Buzz had rushed for 318 yards and had 72 passing yards. The Single-Wing Spartans had made another step. This time he was quite humble when Jesse offered his congratulations. He spent the noisy ride home thinking about next week and the BIG one. Narrows Green Wave would be visiting Spartan territory. He didn't plan to be an accommodating host.

Monday and Tuesday were tough. There had been only four extra runs up the hill. Three for penalties and one for a turnover. Coach Stevens ran another 15 minutes of offensive drills on Monday and 30 extra minutes of defense on Tuesday. He did give the players a ten-minute break after hitting the sled. More to recover himself, after nearly getting his leg broke, than sympathy for the team.

Buzz, Grogan, Gordon, and Mace huddled on their backs in the only grass available just outside the goal post on the practice field. The usually lush turf on the playing portion had a tendency to disappear about this time of year and after weeks of abuse.

"I swear I never saw him fall," Grogan said with a worried look on his face.

"Well, we were running the play behind the line hitting the sled. It wasn't our fault." Gordon replied.

"I thought it was funny." Mace broke in. "He shouldn't have been out in front of the sled – especially, if he's gonna give them big linemen hell the whole time they are working their butts off."

"You think everything's funny, Mace. He could've been hurt bad if Coach Lowery hadn't been riding the sled and seen him go down and blown the whistle." Grogan replied.

"Well, it just got his legs, and I think he's all right. I shouldn't have skipped lunch. I'm hungry as hell." Gordon was always hungry.

Mace snatched a grasshopper out of mid-flight and offered it to him. When Gordon refused, Mace tore off the wings and plopped it into his own mouth.

When the brown juice started dripping out of the corner of Mace's mouth and he pulled out a crooked leg, Gordon gagged and headed toward the water bucket. Buzz and Grogan doubled over with laughter.

"You're crazy, Man." Buzz gave his friend/foe a sharp high-five.

"I bet he's not hungry now." Mace grinned.

Coach Stevens watched the scene from mid-field where he had been conferring with his assistants and rubbing his leg. He smiled as he turned away. Leave it to Mace, the head hunter, to shed a little humor on a difficult day. Stevens knew his boys. They were a tight-knit group and a lot of them had played together since their Little League days. Grogan, the captain, was a leader, and serious. Buzz was a competitor, aggressive and confident. Then there was Mace. The head-hunter who loved to hit, an instigator and a clown.

A teammate had little time to brood or get down on himself with Mace around. He would find him with a cut-down block or rib-breaking tackle and while he had him down, Mace would rub salt into the wound or dust into his eyes. When the poor kid got up, he would be a head-hunter himself, looking for the wide-grinning head of Mace.

A loud whistle and a lap around the field kept Coach Stevens in charge. Sometimes he would be a little slow on the whistle, because he knew how valuable the diversion was. At any rate, by the time of

Thursday's pre-game practice, everyone seemed to be on the same page and focused on Friday night's game.

Buzz was ready for the loudest-of-all pep rallies. What he had not anticipated was what he saw in the hallways of Giles High School on Friday morning. The decorations started in the lobby and continued to Coach Stevens' math room at the other end of the building. Ribbons and balloons hung from the walls and ceiling. Banners and posters were everywhere.

"Beat Narz!" "Sink the Waves" "Go Spartans"

Buzz realized the spirit at Giles had improved, but he didn't expect this display for the third game of the season. Sure, it was the county rivalry, but it wasn't the playoffs or nothing.

Jesse knew it was more than a game. Giles vs Narrows was THE game of the season. He and Shakey were in line at the ticket booth right behind Rocky and Alvin. Jesse preferred seats around the 30-yard line.

He understood that most of the game was never played in the middle of the field. The Hill Gang was gathering to their left. They enjoyed the game in a different fashion than Jesse and Shakey. The Hill Gang's destiny was to harass the refs and players on the other team and second-guess coaches on both sidelines.

Jesse felt a peck on his shoulder. He turned around and shook hands with old-man Kelsey, from over near Newport. Kelsey and his neighbor Ernie had slipped in and taken a seat behind Jesse and Shakey. Ernie was wearing a faded and worn red Spartan jacket. Those jackets hadn't been sold that long ago, so Jesse concluded it was not just for game nights. Ernie probably wore it putting up hay all summer long.

"How many people do you think will be here, Jesse?" Kelsey asked.

"About nine or ten thousand or so, I'd guess."

"Ah, Jesse, they ain't that many people in all of Giles County."

"Well, Kelsey, they ain't all from the county. That lady down there said she drove down from Roanoke. Took a half-day off from work, she said. She's some kind of kin to Rodney, our nose-guard."

Ernie spoke up. "Them three guys down there in the third row drove up from Charlotte, North Carolina. I talked to them over at the Bandana Bar when I was getting a cup of coffee. They said they'd been up a couple of other times just to watch the Spartans practice. It seems like they're Single-Wing old-timers. The old feller said he'd been a tailback in college."

"If they like the Single-Wing and want to see it run right, this is the place to be." Shakey hadn't missed a game in three years and very few practices.

"Ernie don't know much about it." Kelsey said. "I told him he'd better be careful cause it can sure get in your blood."

"Don't worry. I'm sure Shakey will be happy to let him know what's happening. He'll probably draw out a few plays on the back of his program before the night's over with." Jesse said.

Shakey didn't waste any time. "Look here, Ernie. The Spartans line up in an unbalanced line. The quarterback becomes a hard nose blocking-back lined over the tackle. The wing-back lines up outside the end, and you've got one hell-of-a power play off the right side."

"So, they just out-man the other team, Shakey?"

"No, Ernie. That's just part of the Single-Wing. When the other team adjusts and stops the power play, then you throw in the deception. Coach Stevens runs the Straight, the Buck, and the Spin series. When you think you know who is carrying the ball and it turns out to be somebody else, you probably just saw the Buck or Spin moves."

Jesse and Kelsey sat back and enjoyed the game. Ernie would get his education.

"Do you reckon we've got a chance this year, Jesse?"

"I hope so, Kelsey. Narrows has a pretty good team and they beat us 28-13 last year. It can't be nothing like that 48-0 whipping we took two years ago."

Well, it wasn't two years ago, or even last year. The final score was Giles 16, Narrows 0.

When Jesse and Shakey parted ways with their buddies, they could see Ernie diagraming plays in the palm of his hand for old-man Kelsey. Ernie's cows would probably starve next week as they pictured Ernie down at the general store, sitting beside the wood stove with other farmers, explaining the mystery of the Single-Wing.

14

PLAYOFF TIME

The rest of the 1980 season passed much too quickly for Jesse and Buzz, but also to great enjoyment and satisfaction. Jesse recorded each score on his schedule hanging in the kitchen, and Buzz saw another step, a printout of a footprint, posted on the wall in the lobby of Giles High School. The score was printed in large magic marker numbers in the middle of each step.

Giles	16	Parry McCluer	15
Giles	35	James River	7
Giles	16	Narrows	0
Giles	27	Blacksburg	7
Giles	35	Radford	0
Giles	27	George Wythe	0
Giles	28	Christiansburg	20
Giles	34	Roanoke Catholic	6
Giles	38	Carroll County	7
Giles	51	Galax	14

With the exception of Parry McCluer and Christiansburg, Giles had won with ease. The Spartans and the Single-Wing had outscored their opponents 307 points to 76 points. They were undefeated in the regular season.

They were awesome is what they were. By the end of the season, coaches were calling coaches throughout the New River District.

"Coach, what can you tell me about this Giles team?"

"Not much, Coach. They whipped our butts pretty bad."

"What's the best way to defend that Single-Wing offense, Coach? I see they're gaining over 300 yards a game."

"I can't tell you how to stop the Single-Wing, Coach. I can tell you what not to do. Don't overplay the strong side, or they'll kill you on the wing-back reverse or the spin move. Don't bring up your corners, or what looks like a tailback sweep will end up a tailback pass for a touchdown."

"Sounds tough, Coach. How did you prepare for Giles?"

"We wasted three days of practice. You can't duplicate the Single Wing in such short time. We even had our coaches running the plays, and they messed it up. Coach,

you'll be better off working on your offense
and hope you can out score them."

Coach Stevens wasn't making phone
calls, but he was watching a lot of film. Giles
was in the playoffs for the first time in school
history. It had already been a fantastic year.
Everything from here on out was "icing on the
cake". He was determined to do everything
he could to make the dream last as long as it
could.

Buzz was jolted out of his daydreaming with a sharp blare from the PA
system. Every kid should live in his dream
world. He had read *The Roanoke Times*
article on the bulletin board that had his name
in it. He was in several of the pictures of the
game that surrounded the article. The Pep
Club and cheerleaders had mentioned the
Spartans in poems they wrote and read over
the PA in the morning announcements. Now
it was songs. He listened to the cheerleaders'
version of:

YOU GOTTA' LOVE THAT

A PLAY-OFF GAME, AND THE
STANDS PACKED.

FILLED WITH FE-VER, READY TO
AT-TACK.

RED BAN-DAN-AS, AND SPAR-
TAN HATS.

SINGLE-WING FOOT-BALL, YOU
GOTTA' LOVE THAT.

GILES RODE INTO TOWN, PLAYS
IN A SACK.

AN OLD OF-FENSE, ON A ONE
WAY TRACK.

WE'RE TAK-ING A VOW, AIN'T
TURN-ING BACK.

WE KNOW WHAT WE WANT, AND
YOU GOTTA' LOVE THAT.

CAME THOUGH THE SEASON,
WITH A 10 AND 0.

NOW IT'S PLAY-OFF TIME,
WATCH THE SPAR-TANS GO.

IT HAP-PENS EVERY YEAR, THE
SPAR-TANS COME BACK.

IT'S A GILES TRA-DITION, YOU
GOTTA LOVE THAT.

GILES RODE INTO TOWN

PLAYS IN A SACK. AN OLD OF-
FENSE ON A ONE WAY TRACK.

WE'RE TAK-ING A VOW, AIN'T
TURN-ING BACK.

WE KNOW WHAT WE WANT, AND
YOU GOTTA' LOVE THAT.

The head coach of Grundy wasn't
singing. He was worried. The best he could
do would be to bring in Jim. He was the only

one the coach could find that knew how the Single-Wing worked.

"Big-Foot" Jim from over near Birchleaf knew how it worked. He had played blocking-back in the Single-Wing offense for the Cornhuskers. He was nearly 70 years old, but he knew the Single-Wing hadn't changed. Coach Stevens would be using what his dad had taught him and his dad probably got it from Keuffel. Big-Foot had read that book, too.

Big-Foot lined up Grundy's second team in the Single-Wing formation. The head coach took the first-team defense and shifted them over to match the unbalanced line. Big-Foot called for the spin 62 play. The ball never got to the tailback. He called for Buck 38, and the fullback ran over the blocking-back. Big-Foot picked up the fumble and called the reverse. The head coach helped Big-Foot assist the tailback and wing-back off the field after they collided head-on.

When he called 42 pitch, and the defensive end picked off the pitch and ran for a touchdown the other way, Big-Foot just stood there shaking his head. It sure worked a lot better in the old days.

The head coach decided to call it a day. They would just line up and go after the Spartan with the ball. Big Foot walked away. He knew that, with Giles, the guy with the ball wouldn't be the guy with the ball. He and his buddies, Harley, Snake, and old-man Josh, had kept up with Giles through the newspaper, and they would be at the game Friday night. Rooting for the Golden Wave, but watching the Spartans.

Coach Stevens pulled the tape of the pre-season scrimmage against Grundy and witnessed again how equally matched the two teams were. The Cole kid for the Golden Wave was surely a college prospect. He figured the Spartans, maybe, could stop Cole; he just hoped that Grundy couldn't stop the Single-Wing.

Grundy couldn't and Grundy didn't. The final score was Giles 31, Grundy 0.

On Monday, Coach Stevens noticed the addition to the "one-step-at-a-time" display in the lobby. The footprint was much larger than those of the regular season. He thought how appropriate it was. Each step in the playoffs would be a big step. Each game would be against better and better competition as the weaker teams were eliminated. With more than a hundred AA schools in Virginia, it was quite an honor to be one of the top ten.

He didn't have time to dwell in his pride and glory. He had a battle to prepare for and troops to get ready. Abingdon would be marching into Spartan grounds on Friday night. The scouts had done a good job and he had film to break down. His twelve-hour days were now running about 16. It was a chance of a lifetime.

It seemed like a lifetime to Buzz. The week was the same - three hard days of practice, film of Abingdon, and more songs, poems, and news articles. The big difference was the intensity. Spirit in the school was overflowing, but the team went through their paces in a somber, quiet, methodical ritual. Even Mace couldn't conjure up a prank to break the spell.

Buzz wasn't worried. He just couldn't wait. The knot in his stomach would only go away when he got his hands on the football and took that first hit in the game. Everything would be OK after that.

Jesse thought it was better than OK. He thought it was super as he handed Buzz his hotdog and drink after the game.

"Twelve down and two to go, Buzz." Jesse smiled.

"What happened to that one step at a time?" Buzz noticed the damp bandana around Jesse's neck. He had either mopped up some liquid or had done a little perspiring.

The final score was Giles 21, Abingdon 14.

Now there were only four teams left. Buzz waited Monday morning as the PA system dispensed with the regular announcements. Few of the students stopped their constant chattering until the music started. All ears were alert to the cheerleaders' new rendition that would have made Elvis proud.

TAKING CARE OF BUSINESS

WE GET UP EVERY MORNING, IF IT'S SUNNY OR STORMING

TAKE THE OLD YELLOW BUS TO THE SCHOOL

THERE'S A WHISTLE UP ABOVE US, PLAYERS PUSHING PLAYERS SHOVING

AND THE COACHES WHO TRY TO STAY COOL.

AND IF YOU AIN'T ON TIME, OR IF YOU GET FAR BEHIND

YOU BETTER HUSTLE AND BE ON
YOUR WAY

IF THE COACH GETS ANNOYED,
YOU MAY BE UN-EMPLOYED

HE JUST LOVES TO PRACTICE
HARD ALL DAY.

WE'VE BEEN TAKING CARE OF
BUSINESS, EVERY DAY

TAKING CARE OF BUSINESS,
EVERY WAY

WE'VE BEEN TAKING CARE OF
BUSINESS, IT'S ALL RIGHT

TAKING CARE OF BUSINESS, AND
WINNING FRIDAY NIGHT.

The Spartans did take care of business,
but it wasn't Friday night. It was Saturday
afternoon when the black uniforms of
Jefferson Forest darkened the field of Spartan
Stadium. Mother Nature had decided to join

in with cold weather and blowing snow. It was not to be an omen for Giles.

The final score was Giles 30, Jefferson Forest 21.

15

DEALING WITH SPIES

The Virginia State AA Championship was to be played on the Giles Spartans' own field. Coach Ryder of Park-View Sterling didn't like that idea much, but it would give his players a chance to get out of the Northern Virginia suburbs and see some of the country west of the Blue Ridge Mountains. It probably wouldn't hurt to share a little of the Nation's Capital culture with the Spartans of the Appalachian Mountains.

Coach Ryder had little concern of leaving the state championship trophy in those mountains. After all, he had the premier running back in the country. He didn't know

it at the time, but Allen Phillips, his star
tailback, would soon set records at Notre
Dame and later play in the NFL. He did know
that there was no way the Cinderella team of
Giles could match up with Park-View
Sterling.

Coach Ryder was still a coach. Since
he had not scouted Giles and had not obtained
a film, he decided to send two of his JV
coaches down to Pearisburg to watch a couple
of practices. He gave them a Giles roster he
had received in the mail and told them he
wanted a report by Thursday so he could get
in a pre-game practice with the team.

It took Coaches Dillon and Lewis two
days to get to Giles. They knew they were in
Spartan Country when they crossed Brush
Mountain just west of Blacksburg. The signs
told them so. The first one didn't say
"Welcome to Giles County", instead it was
more of a warning. "You are Entering
Spartan Territory." Red bandanas hung from
trees or signpost every quarter mile. "Go
Spartans", "Beat Park-View Sterling", "Giles

1", "Go Big Red", and many more signs were posted from stop signs, store marquees, and front yards along route 460 from Newport to Giles High School.

The scouts left Hardee's and shook their heads as they again passed store after store with Spartan signs and banners. The Giles Shoe Center was something to behold. Dillon wanted to go in and buy a pair of red bandana boots. Lewis squelched the notion, pointing out it might look like he was a bit of a traitor back in Northern Virginia.

Lewis motioned to a huge star on the side of Angels Rest Mountain with a glowing red "1".

"Wonder what the "1" stands for?" he asked.

"Probably the number of red lights in Pearisburg. I've only seen one." smiled Dillon.

When they drove onto the high school campus, they passed a sign that read, "Welcome to Giles High School – Spartan Spirit and Spartan Pride". Sheets with slogans and footballs with a single wing attached marking the Spartans' victories through the New River District and Region IV were hanging from the top floor windows and flapping in the breeze.

When the scouts passed the entrance to Spartan Stadium, heading up to the practice field, they saw a huge red "Single-Wing football" with a big "G" outlined with blinking lights attached to the side of the press box.

"They sure got a thing going with this football that looks like half a bird, don't they, Coach?"

"It's their trademark for their offense. Remember Coach Ryder said that Giles ran some kind of ancient offense called the Single-Wing."

Mixing in with the crowd that was watching practice wasn't very difficult for the spies. They had missed the warm-ups and arrived just as the offensive drills began.

Lewis and Dillon exchanged puzzled looks as they stared at the weird formation. Dillon quickly diagrammed it on a clipboard he had tucked in the back of his pants and under his coat. Lewis smiled as he watched the long snap from center to the tailback.

"That should be good for a few turnovers," he whispered to Dillon.

As practice wore on, his smile faded, and the raised-eyebrows look of appreciation became frequent between the scouts as the center made perfect snaps to the tailback. The handoffs to the blocking-back and the wing-back at full speed worked as smoothly as passing a thread through a needle. The scouts lost the ball in the exchange most of the time. The tailback could pin-point a pass on the run, or drop back and plant his feet for the deep bomb. The outsiders could not tell when a sweep would end up as a ten-yard pass to a trailing end.

The double-team blocking and traps opened gaping holes in the defensive line. Lewis and Dillon were impressed. Maybe the Spartans' weakness would be their defense. This Single-Wing offense wasn't the kind of news they wanted to take back to Coach Ryder.

After an hour of hard-hitting offense, the scouts were afforded the agony of watching harder-hitting defense. All of the linemen came low and hard. They split double teams and closed down traps. The left end (Mace) couldn't be blocked, and the strong side linebacker (Carl) was everywhere!

As the two-hour practice was ending, disbelief swept over the scouts. Everything they had seen was live. Nothing like the practices they were used to. Dillon didn't see a blocking dummy on the field.

The Spartans weren't through. Fifty-some players lined up across the field, head-to-head, and one-on-one. On the cadence, they hit. They hit crushing blows with legs pumping, even when a player went down, until Coach Stevens blew the whistle. After several minutes of one-on-one, they jogged up to the edge of a steep hill. The scouts flinched in pain as they watched fourth-quarter legs sprint up the "mountain".

The spies had had enough. They started easing off of the practice field. The Giles Spartans didn't practice for a game – they prepared for war. Coach Ryder would not be pleased.

As they headed out the gate, a runner caught up with them.

"Coach Stevens wants to know if you could hang around. He said to tell you he would be happy to show you the school."

Embarrassed, the spies hung around.

Coach Stevens introduced himself and his assistants. Coaches Lewis and Dillon did the same. Coach Stevens smiled as he opened the locker room door and invited the scouts into his office for some coffee and reminiscing. It had been a great year for both teams. Undefeated, and battling Saturday for the state championship.

Lewis glanced up as he entered the red and blue locker room. He and Dillon, unbeknownst to them, were being given the privilege of seeing what only Spartan Varsity players would ever have the opportunity to see. The Spartan "Wall of Fame". On the wall hung the pictures of a half-dozen of

Giles' best with a label of their honors.
Where dozens would eventually hang, were
All-District, All-Region, and for now, one
All-State. Not bad for the short three-year
tenure of Coach Stevens. No doubt, there
would be several additions from this year's
successful team.

Dillon couldn't help but smile when he
stepped into the toilet and saw the beginning
of a monument of lesser stature. The names
of obviously every player and their number
was etched in the black slate partition of the
stall. No one had bothered to remove or paint
over the scribe, and now it was anchored in as
one of the many Spartan Single-Wing
traditions.

Coach Stevens offered the scouts some
of the cookies and apples that filled boxes on
his desk. "Compliments of the Boosters," he
told them, "as well as the ribbons, poster, and
banners decorating the locker room."

Coach Stevens showed Lewis and
Dillon the locker room that Park-View
Sterling would be using. He introduced them

to the athletic director and took them through the main hall of Giles to meet the principal.

The hallway was of little surprise after all the scouts had seen. Hundreds of red ribbons were tied to the lockers, banners were hanging from the ceiling, and every classroom door was decorated. The Spartan bulletin board, recognizing the last battle, received a little more of the scouts' attention. Before Coach Stevens released the scouts for a safe trip home, he gave them a couple of video tapes of the Single-Wing in action.

Coaches Lewis and Dillon were nearly back to Roanoke before they had gathered their thoughts enough to break the doomsday silence. Park-View was a good football team, and they had the record to prove it. They had taken on many good teams and come away victorious. They had never taken on a whole county!

Lewis knew he would never be able to explain the Single-Wing to Coach Ryder. The more he saw, the more he had become confused.

"How did he know we were scouts?" asked Dillon.

"Why would he give us a game film?"

A lot of things were weird. Both of the spies would be glad when they got on the East side of the Blue Ridge Mountains.

16

STATE CHAMPIONSHIP

Jesse woke up before daybreak. He
was sitting in his rocker on the front porch
with a blanket wrapped around his shoulders
when the sunlight began penetrating the dark
gray crest of Butt Mountain. He saw the
silhouette of Buzz meander out on the stoop of
his house down the street. The boy couldn't
sleep either. It was his big day, and maybe the
biggest day in his lifetime. Jesse realized
there would be more important days in the
boy's life, but maybe none would be as
memorable.

Buzz would have to be at the school at
9:00 for breakfast. Coach Stevens didn't want
the team to lie around in bed until game time.
He wanted a regular routine as much as

possible and that meant getting up, eating a good breakfast, and relaxing.

Jesse would take the boys to breakfast, but there was plenty of time for him and Buzz to take a ride over to the county line and look at all the signs that had been posted along Route 460. He grabbed his coat, picked up his camera, and headed for the car. He had four rolls of film and he intended to record as much of this historic day as he could.

After the sight-seeing tour, Jesse and Buzz picked up Grogan. Jesse dropped the boys off at the door of the school cafeteria. He parked on the far side of the parking lot and turned off the engine of the car. He wanted to just sit and absorb all the happenings.

Mr. Pruitt, the principal, had called all his troops together. The fire department was in charge of the parking, state troopers set up orange traffic cones and directed vehicles off Route 460, and county deputies and town police were handling the crowd and would escort the officials on and off the field. Maintenance would guard the press box and the players' gate. Mr. Mitchell and his squad and volunteers were already heating up the coffee and putting on the first batch of hotdogs. Teachers were taking their places to sell and take up tickets. Administrators were running all over the place. Rocky and Alvin arrived.

Coach Stevens was frustrated. Two good drives had been stopped with turnovers. The great Spartan crowd was stunned. The usually-waving red bandanas had all but wilted away and disappeared in the silent hands of the Giles crowd. The Hill Gang started some Monday morning coaching.

"Throw the ball!"

"Are you crazy, Coach. Run 32 Buck!"

Just before half-time, Allen Phillips had scored three touchdowns and Park-View Sterling was leading the game 18-0. But, with just a few minutes to go in the second quarter, Buzz took off for a 74 yard touchdown. After finally stopping Phillips, and with only seconds left in the half, Buzz again started off the right side, but pulled up and threw a pass to a wide-open Gordon in the end zone. All of a sudden, Giles was back in the ballgame, and went in at halftime trailing 18-14.

Jesse knew that Phillips was good, but so was Cole of Grundy. What was wrong with the Spartans?

Coach Stevens' choices of words at halftime are not printable. The destruction of the classroom in the Ag building where the Spartans were sequestered is not important. Mr. Shelton hardly ever used that podium anyway.

When Coach Stevens decided he'd sufficiently replaced the fear of Park-View, he began diagramming x's and o's on the blackboard. Sometimes the skull session was interrupted with another bout of terror.

"You all don't have to be SCARED anymore about Park-View. You don't need to be SCARED of losing this football game. You have pretty much taken care of that."

Another cup of water hit the window across the room. A few minutes of silence as he eyeballed each and every player. One player failed to meet his stare. Coach Stevens stomped over, grasped the player underneath his should pads, lifted him to his feet, and, nose-to-nose and eyeball-to-eyeball, asked him.

"Are you ashamed to be a Giles Spartan, Robbie?"

"No... Sir."

"Then why in the hell are you hanging your head?"

Coach Stevens politely and gently set the trembling player back down in his chair. He moved back to the front of the room and stood a few seconds facing his x's and o's.

When he turned back around, the demon in his face was gone and he spoke in his most serious and prophetic tone.

"Men, we're not supposed to win this game. We're not even supposed to be here. We've had a great season, and we sure as hell don't have any reason to hang our heads.

"Nobody has worked any harder than you have. You've given me everything I have ever asked for. When I wanted a hundred percent out of you, you gave a hundred and ten.

"No matter how this game turns out, I want every one of you to look me in the eye. I'm damn proud of you!

"There's just one more thing. I'm a SPARTAN. You are all Giles High School Spartans. You are the masters of the best offense in the country – the Single-Wing. There ain't no way that I'm gonna sit on my butt, feeling sorry for myself, and let a bunch of city boys come down here in my own backyard, and take that away from me. Let's go out there and have some fun."

Coach Stevens walked out of the room. He took a cup of water from Coach Edwin.

"What do you think, Coach? Did I get their attention?"

A big roar went up in the classroom as the team put their hands together in a show of solidarity.

"I think you got their attention, Coach."

Phillips scored two more touchdowns in the second half. The five touchdowns would remain a Virginia State Championship record for years to come.

The Spartans were having fun. The bandanas in the stands caught a breeze and were flapping madly. The Hill Gang quit coaching Coach Stevens and began giving lip service to Park-View Sterling. Near the end of the fourth quarter, Giles took the lead for the first time with the score of 33-26.

Park-View had a job to do and a very short time to do it in. With the time running out, they pushed the ball down the field and scored with seconds on the clock. Down by one point, Coach Ryder had a decision to make.

Park-View Sterling could tie the game and force overtime by kicking and making the extra point. They had failed in three previous attempts at kicking for the extra point. If they tied the game, could they hold back the Spartans who showed up as a different team the second half?

On the other hand, Coach Ryder had the best tailback in the country in Allen Phillips. Surely he could carry the whole Giles defense for three yards. Coach Ryder couldn't take the chance on another missed kick or an overtime. He was going for the two- point conversion and a State Championship.

So this was the way it would be – the way it ought to be. Jesse stood with Shakey and the rest of the 10,000-plus fans in the stadium. One play – one State Championship.

Everyone in the world knew who would carry the ball. Giles had Bruce Farley who knew and who got a hand out as he was crushed to the ground with a double-team block. Tripped up and losing his balance, Phillips charged ahead and crashed head-to-head with Carl Martin, the Spartan linebacker that Dillon and Lewis remembered "being everywhere". When the dust settled, the last whistle blew, "Mighty" Phillips was a yard short.

The final score was Giles 33, Park-View Sterling 32.

The Giles High School Spartans were the 1980 Virginia AA State Champions. The crowd would not go home. They swarmed the field, the players, and Coach Stevens. Jesse and Shakey hugged each other with tears in their eyes. The band played "WE ARE THE CHAMPIONS".

THE Coach, standing in his reserved seat in the press box, thought to himself as he gave a thumbs-up to his son down on the field, we are the SINGLE-WING CHAMPIONS.

Author's Notes

Harry Ragsdale (The Coach), Stephen Ragsdale's dad, ran the Single-Wing offense at Narrows High School. The Green Wave compiled five unbeaten seasons under Harry, including a 28-0 record in his last three years on the job.

Coach Stephen C. Ragsdale (Coach Stevens) coached the Spartans of Giles High School for 29 years with a record of 255-88. In his first season, Giles went 2-8. The next year the Spartans finished at 6-3-1. His third year, 1980, Coach Ragsdale led the Spartans to a 14-0 season and won a Group AA State Title in an era when there were only three classifications.

178

Ragsdale went on to lead Giles to two more State Championships in Group A Division 2, in 1993 and 2005, with runner-up finishes in 1996 and 2006. He retired after the 2007 season. Shortly thereafter, the Giles County School Board named the football field where Ragsdale and the Giles High Spartans were so successful running the Single-Wing Offense, "The Stephen C. Ragsdale Field." In 2014, Stephen Ragsdale was inducted into the Virginia High School Hall of Fame.

The legacy is continuing under Coach Jeff Williams, one of the original Single-Wing running backs of the 1980 championship team. As one of Coach Ragsdale's assistant coaches, he helped coach the 1993 and 2005 state champions and the 1996 and 2006 state runners-up. Under Coach Williams, Giles used the Single-Wing in winning the state title in 2013, going 15-0. The Giles Spartans continued their winning streak to 27 games into 2014.

Another of Ragsdale's warriors from the 1980 State Champions, Greg Mance, went on to coach football at Richlands High School. For the past 17 years he has been successful running the more modern version called the

'Spread' Offense, and compiled a record of 160-56. The Richlands Blue Tornados has previously won 10 straight district titles and 2 state championships under Coach Mance.

No, the single-wing is not completely dead. It is still run successfully by a small group of teams across the country, mostly at the high-school level. But few teams have been as successful as the Ragsdales in the County of Giles, Virginia, deep in the Appalachian Mountains.

CARRY ON, COACH WILLIAMS and THE MIGHTY SPARTANS!

ABOUT THE AUTHOR
Vic Edwards

is the author of *Single-Wingin'* and his first novel
Hanger. Both books are available at
Amazon.com . He graduated from Radford
University and taught school in Giles County for
25 years.
He and his wife Sue are now retired from
teaching and live in Bristol, Virginia. They have
three children and six grandchildren.

vicedwards@bvu.net

Vic's son Joe   *Coach Ragsdale*   *Vic*

44075752R00107

Made in the USA
Charleston, SC
14 July 2015